D0788220

ILLICIT NIGHT WITH THE GREEK

ILLICIT NIGHT WITH THE GREEK

BY

SUSANNA CARR

First published in Great Britain 2016
By Mills & Boon, an imprint of HarperCollins*Publishers*
1 London Bridge Street, London, SE1 9GF

Large Print edition 2016

ISBN: 978-0-263-26200-1

Our policy is to use papers that are natural, renewable and recyclable products and made from wood grown in sustainable forests. The logging and manufacturing processes conform to the legal environmental regulations of the country of origin.

Printed and bound in Great Britain
by CPI Antony Rowe, Chippenham, Wiltshire

CHAPTER ONE

TENSION GRIPPED STERGIOS ANTONIOU as he stood alone on the balcony that jutted out from his cousin's mansion. He ignored the iconic view of the Parthenon against the blue September sky as he scowled at the blonde woman at the garden party below.

Jodie Little. His stepsister. His darkest secret.

Burning hot fury ate away at him as he watched Jodie glide through the crowd of Athens's high society. She looked different. She had cut and straightened the long mop of curls. Her hair now fell into soft waves that reached her pointed chin. The yellow floral dress was modest as it skimmed her slender figure. Her bold red lipstick was at odds with her delicate appearance.

He knew the presentable image was false. It was a masquerade, a shield. It had been years since he'd last seen her but he knew time couldn't have tamed her true nature.

"There you are," his mother said as she stood beside him. "When did you get here? Come join the party."

Stergios didn't look away from Jodie. "How long has she been in Greece?" he asked.

Mairi Antoniou sighed. She rested her forearms against the ornate balustrade as she watched her stepdaughter charm a guileless shipping heiress. "She let her father know she was at a nearby hotel about two days ago. If she thought she would be welcomed with open arms, she is going to be extremely disappointed."

"Why has she returned?"

"Something about missing her father."

Stergios studied Jodie intently. The seductress didn't understand the meaning of family. She had been absent from her father's life for four years and she suddenly wanted a reunion. "What do you think is the real reason?"

"I don't know," she replied softly. "Gregory doesn't have money of his own."

"And Jodie recently inherited a fortune," he murmured. He tore his gaze away from Jodie and scanned the sophisticated crowd for her father. Stergios spotted the tall, well-dressed man on the other side of the lush garden.

Gregory Little had a talent for marrying wealthy women. His only goals were to keep his powerful wife happy and live in the luxury she provided. Stergios knew his stepfather was a benign presence in their lives, unlike his daughter.

“Gregory didn’t know she was coming for a visit,” Mairi insisted. “They’ve been in contact after her mother died earlier this year, but he didn’t invite her.”

Stergios’s stepfather was given a generous allowance. The man knew what was expected of him if he wanted to keep the money flowing, but having a wealthy daughter meant another stream of revenue. “Do you believe him?”

“Of course. Jodie has caused him nothing but trouble and embarrassment.” His mother’s voice was brittle with anger. “That girl almost caused a rift in our family because she couldn’t keep her legs closed.”

The blood pounded hard in Stergios’s veins as he remembered. Jodie knew how to create problems with minimum effort. It could be uttering an explosive comment at a formal dinner or creating a public spectacle at Athens's most popular nightclub. But none of that compared to seducing his cousin Dimos. If she had succeeded, it would have destroyed a bright and promising future for the Antoniou family.

"She shouldn't be here," he declared gruffly. Why had she shown up this week of all weeks? "Does Dimos know that she's around?"

Mairi stiffened. "I asked him to put Jodie on the invitation list for this party," she reluctantly admitted.

Stergios cursed as he pushed away from the balustrade. He scanned the guests at the party but he didn't see his cousin. That alone was suspicious. Dimos had always gravitated toward Jodie.

"What happened between them is in the past," his mother argued. "Dimos was in a rebellious stage and was easily misled. He was no match for a determined whore."

Jodie had entranced Dimos almost instantly, yet his cousin had not been an innocent victim. Stergios knew his mother refused to believe that. She'd like to think that an Antoniou man had better standards.

"It took us too long to realize that she was a

manipulative liar," his mother declared. "When she said you'd followed her into the wine cellar that night… Well, no one was going to believe that."

Stergios closed his eyes briefly. Everyone in the family knew about his aversion to dark and confined spaces. But he had pushed past the reluctance that night because of Jodie. Because of her special brand of trouble.

"Of course she couldn't bewitch you, but Dimos was unworldly back then," his mother continued. "Just remembering everything she has done makes me—"

"It's too much of a coincidence that Jodie has returned when we need this alliance with the Volakis family. She's out for revenge."

His mother scoffed at the idea. "She's not the type who would follow the financial news or understand your long-term plans for the Antoniou Group. Jodie is not that smart. For goodness' sake, she's a finishing school dropout."

"Jodie wasn't kicked out of all those schools because of her academic performance," he reminded her.

"She has no interest in destroying us," his mother said. "She wants to *be* one of us."

"Sometimes the enemy is within the family."

Silence pulsed between them. Stergios inhaled sharply as he firmly pushed back the memories. He sensed his mother turning to face him. Stergios mastered his troubled thoughts and didn't flinch when she tentatively placed her hand against his shoulder.

"You don't need to protect us against Jodie." Concern wavered in her voice.

His mother was wrong. He must always remain alert. Build enough power and wealth that nothing could touch them. He didn't want anyone in his family to know the bleak and cruel world he had experienced.

"She's a problem but we've dealt with worse. In fact, we won't need to do anything," Mairi said brightly, dropping her hand before she turned away. "Jodie can't pretend to be demure and innocent for long. Her true colors will show. They always do."

"And while we wait, she'll seduce Dimos and stop the wedding," he predicted.

His mother gasped. “No, Dimos won’t betray us like that.”

“Dimos will bed Jodie the first chance he gets,” he countered. He knew his cousin would view Jodie as the one who got away.

“He won’t,” she argued. “He knows how important this merger is to the family.”

That didn’t stop Dimos four years ago, Stergios thought grimly. If anything, the need to claim Jodie was more imperative to his cousin now. But Mairi Antoniou had a blind spot when it came to family. It was his duty to recognize and eliminate any threats.

“Jodie knows the importance, as well,” he warned as he grasped his mother’s elbow and guided her back to the party. “She has returned because she has some unfinished business and the money to fund it. She’s a real threat to the Antoniou-Volakis marriage. We need this alliance and I won’t let Jodie Little destroy it.”

Some things never change, Jodie told herself. She flashed a friendly smile at one of the older Antoniou women. The curmudgeon in unrelieved black didn’t reciprocate as she drew the lovely heiress away to the other side of the garden. It was as if this family believed Jodie could corrupt the young woman with just her presence.

She strolled along the garden, sipping from her water glass as if she didn't feel all eyes on her. Jodie knew she was being paranoid. Many of the relatives had been indifferent to her when she had lived in Athens. Yet no one seemed happy that she had returned.

Jodie sensed a strange undercurrent that hung in the late summer breeze. These people were convinced she was going to make a mistake or cause a scandal. It was as if the Antoniou family was waiting for disaster and bracing themselves for impact.

They were in for a long wait. Jodie locked her smile into place. That was the old Jodie. She was wiser now, and more in control of her emotions. This time she was determined to fit in. She straightened her shoulders and took a deep breath, inhaling the fragrant garden flowers. This time she would belong.

"Jodie?"

She gave a start when she recognized the male voice. She whirled around and saw her cousin

Dimos Antoniou. Jodie instinctively took a step back and wished she hadn't shown any sign of weakness. She corrected herself and welcomed him with a smile before he embraced her with a strong hug.

"It has been so long," Dimos said as he kissed both her cheeks.

"It has," she agreed, not allowing his touch to linger. He looked exactly as she remembered, with his long face, lanky build and black hair that flopped over his forehead. "Thank you for inviting me to your new home. It's beautiful."

"Zoi's family gave it to us as a wedding present."

"I think you and your fiancée will be very happy here."

He thrust his hands in his pockets and rocked back on his feet. "Can you imagine me getting married?" he asked.

She silently shook her head. Dimos was three years older and she had been grateful for his friendship, but he had always seemed immature for his age. "And you're a vice president with the Antoniou Group."

He ducked his head. "That won't be official until I come back from my honeymoon."

"Your family is very proud of you and they want you to have the best of everything. You deserve it," she said huskily as the words caught in her throat. Dimos had understood the rules very early on and, more importantly, had followed them. In return, he was rewarded handsomely.

She wondered what it was like to be loved and accepted by family. She wanted that now more than ever. Jodie had yearned for a wisp of connection with her parents but she had waited for them to make the first move. She now regretted her lack of action when her mother had died suddenly of a heart attack several months ago. Jodie knew she had to do something immediately if she wanted to have a relationship with her father, her only living relative. She would have to be the first to apologize, to yield, to change.

But what kind of sacrifices would she have to make to have her father accept her? How much would she have to hide about herself to be considered lovable?

Dimos's smile dipped as the light dimmed from

his eyes. "That's very kind of you, Jodie. Especially after what happened between us."

Shock washed over her and she fought for a mildly interested expression. She hadn't been prepared for Dimos—for any Antoniou—to mention that night. Jodie wanted to cross her arms and back away but she was immobile. The only thing she felt was the pressure of her fingertips as they pressed against the cool surface of her water glass.

Dimos shoved his hand in his hair and looked away. "I did not handle the situation well," he confessed in a low tone.

She fought the urge to find a quick getaway. "No one did," she mumbled. She had been branded a Jezebel, a woman determined to snag an Antoniou man for a husband and ruin any potential marriages that had been carefully orchestrated. After that night she had been considered extremely dangerous to the Antoniou family's future.

"I didn't know that one of the maids had seen us."

Jodie blinked. That was what he was apologizing for? That they had been caught? Interrupted?

She pressed her lips together before she said anything. It was tempting to give a scathing reply but she had to be on her best behavior.

"I couldn't believe that maid went and told Stergios." Bitter anger bloomed in Dimos's voice. "What had she been thinking?"

Jodie wondered if she might bite her tongue off as she fought back the words. The maid had known exactly what Dimos's intentions had been. Jodie wished she had figured it out earlier. She had seen Dimos as a cousin who helped her navigate a big family, not as a viable lover.

"And I know this is years too late, but I should have spoken up." Dimos splayed out his hands. "I didn't realize you would have been severely punished."

She was wrong, Jodie decided. Dimos was still immature for his age. Her jaw hurt as she fought to remain silent and took a small sip from her water glass. She wanted to point out that she had never encouraged him, or that it was never too late to right a wrong. He could have protected her from the fallout at any time. But that wouldn't have served him.

And if there was something she had learned

over the years, especially after that infamous night, it was that men didn't understand the meaning of honor, respect or protection. They pursued, they took what they could get and they got out fast.

"So, how long are you planning to stay in Greece?" Dimos asked with a puzzled expression when she didn't respond.

She darted a glance at her father standing among the older Antoniou men. Her first goal was to ask for forgiveness for her past behavior but she didn't know if her father would give her the chance. "I'm not sure," she murmured. "My plans aren't set in stone."

"Then you must come to my wedding," he said, his eyes widening with enthusiasm.

Jodie raised her hand to halt that line of thinking. "I don't want to intrude."

"Intrude?" Dimos laughed. "That's not possible. You're family."

She wished it were true. She wished she didn't have this need to belong somewhere. To belong with someone. She had always been the outsider. The burden. She was used to it, and at times wore the label like a badge of honor, but everything changed after her mother's death. She wanted to be loved, accepted and part of a family.

"You must agree," Dimos insisted.

"Jodie must agree to what?"

She went still when she heard the low, masculine voice. Stergios Antoniou was here. She swallowed hard. He was standing next to her. Her pulse began to gallop as her stomach made a sickening turn. Her skin went hot and then cold but she refused to look in his direction.

"I invited her to my wedding," Dimos said with a touch of defiance.

"I doubt there's space," Stergios responded.

"I can make space," Dimos promised Jodie. "It's going to be on an island that Zoi's family owns. It's small, but not that small."

She nervously licked her lips as the panic swelled inside her. It pressed against her skin, ready to burst free. Every instinct told her to run but she stood as still as a statue. "I wouldn't want to cause any inconvenience for you or your bride," she explained huskily.

"You won't," Dimos said with a lopsided smile. "I'll go ask Zoi right now."

She watched helplessly as Dimos strode toward his fiancée. She wanted to run and hide but knew she had to be brave. At least appear fearless. From the corner of her eye, she saw Stergios's crisp white linen suit. She forced herself to turn. Jodie looked straight ahead at his pale blue shirt. She tried to ignore how it emphasized the breadth of his powerful chest before she jerked her gaze to his face.

Her breath snagged in her throat as her heartbeat roared in her ears. She stared at Stergios's luxuriant black hair that fell past his chin. The shadow of a dark beard almost diminished the whitened scar on his upper lip.

This was not the Stergios she'd known. She blinked several times, noting the bold lines of his cheekbones and nose, the slash of his mouth and his warm golden skin. She recalled how he'd once kept his hair ruthlessly short and had shaved twice a day. Now it looked as if he could no longer contain the wildness that rumbled through him.

His dark brown eyes were cold as he callously assessed her and immediately found her lacking. "I don't know what you're trying to achieve—"

"I wasn't asking for an invite," she bit out. "He offered and wouldn't take no for an answer."

"Perhaps he didn't understand what you were saying." His gaze drifted to her mouth. "You're not good at saying no to any man."

She swallowed the gasp of outrage and fought the driving need to fling the contents of her glass into his face. Damn it, her new and improved image was already slipping. She was never in control when she was around her stepbrother. She had to get away from Stergios or risk making a scene. That wouldn't help her gain forgiveness from her father.

"Don't confuse me with the women you associate with." Jodie turned on her heel.

"Running away already?"

She whipped around, wobbling to a standstill as she glared at him. Stergios had sounded disinterested and bored while she was a jittery mass of nerves. It wasn't fair. "I don't run away. That's your signature move, stepbrother dear."

The muscle bunching in his cheek was the only indication that her barb had hit its target. "You know how to create a disaster and leave without a trace while everyone else deals with the aftermath. The merger had fallen apart after that night because Dimos suddenly didn't want to get married. It has taken me years just to get the Antoniou-Volakis wedding to this point."

"I was banished." She wanted to stamp her feet. This was bad. It was as if her hard-earned poise had disintegrated into nothing. "There's a difference."

"Banished?" Stergios repeated with skepticism. "You've always been dramatic."

And you've always been cold and hateful. No, she realized that wasn't true. Stergios had been tolerant the first time she'd moved in with the Antoniou family. He had been her only companion, her one true confidant. But gradually he had become distant.

The more he was around her, the more he knew and learned about her, the more hostile he became. It had been a relief and yet agony when he missed her eighteenth birthday to work overseas on a project. He had returned a few months later but her joy had been brief and misplaced. It had become obvious that Stergios couldn't stand being in the same room with her.

"If you were banished, why are you working so

hard to return to the family fold?" His tone was casual but he watched her with open suspicion. "You're not the type to forgive."

Stergios knew her too well. Having one person understand her should bring comfort, but this man would use that knowledge against her. "I am here," she said slowly, emphasizing each word, "to repair my relationship with my father."

"And that's all?"

No, this time she wanted Gregory Little's concern and interest. She wanted to be a priority. She'd always wanted that from her father but she had tried to gain it the wrong way when she had been a teenager.

Jodie lifted her head when she suddenly understood Stergios's question. "Oh…you think I'm here to get revenge or to cause trouble. To stop this merger that you need so badly. I hate to disappoint you, but the Antoniou family isn't worth my time."

One winged eyebrow arched at her statement. As if he couldn't believe his family wasn't everyone's top interest. "You returned just when Dimos and Zoi are about to marry."

"I'm sorry I didn't get the family newsletter,"

she said with exaggerated sweetness, "or I would have timed my visit better."

She was about to flounce away but Stergios easily read her next move. He grabbed her arm, his large fingers biting into her pale flesh as he held her still. Her skin went hot as she remembered the last time he touched her. She knew better than to look at him or she would betray her conflicted emotions.

"I don't trust you." His voice was low against her ear.

She shivered from his nearness. "I don't care."

Stergios's grasp tightened. "Stay away from Dimos."

"With pleasure," she said in a hiss and forced herself to look into his dark eyes. "Now let go of me."

Jodie saw the turbulent emotions chasing across his face before he abruptly released her. She was uncomfortably aware how her skin tingled from his touch. "I have no interest in Dimos," she continued. "I didn't seduce him back then and I'm not pursuing him now."

"Why should I believe you? You're a liar."

Her anger flashed wildly. Yes, she had lied in

the past, but it had been a stupid and instinctual attempt to protect Stergios that night. She had made a sacrifice for him and he couldn't see it, couldn't appreciate it. The hurt and the injustice of it all rolled inside her. "And if I wanted to seduce Dimos, there is nothing you could do about it," she slung at him.

"I'm warning you, Jodie." His voice was low and menacing.

She pressed her lips together. Why did she say that? Why was she provoking Stergios? She knew better but she was unable to stop. "I could have had him in my bed like that." She gave a satisfying snap with her fingers. "I certainly wouldn't have picked a cold wall in a dark wine cellar."

They stared at each other, instantly trapped in the inconvenient memories. She shifted, her spine aching as she remembered the rough brick against her back. Jodie swallowed as she recalled how she had laved her tongue against Stergios's warm skin. She felt her cheeks flush as the echoes of their mingled gasps and incoherent words reverberated in her mind.

She couldn't think about that. Not now, not here, not ever. "I could have contacted Dimos any time over the years," she declared in a rush. "And he would have dropped everything for the chance to have sex with me."

Stergios sneered with disgust. "So you know the power you have over him."

She did now, not when she had been eighteen. "I know the power I have over all men," she said loftily. "Dimos is more susceptible than most."

"And why do you think that is?"

No doubt he saw it as her fault. "I haven't encouraged him at all, but warn me off again," she said in a growl as she glared at him, "and all bets are off."

Stergios braced his legs as if he was preparing for battle. "You dare to threaten me?"

"There is very little I wouldn't dare," she told him boldly as her legs shook. "I am here to be with my father. If you block that in any way, I will do everything in my power to stop the Antoniou-Volakis merger."

His expression went blank. There was no anger or repulsion. It was like a mask and that unsettled Jodie more than his cold fury.

"It wouldn't take much." She knew she had to stop talking and yet she pursed her lips and made a show of looking around the party. “All I have to do is crook my finger and Dimos will—”

“You have always been a destructive force.” His voice was just a rasp. “But I won’t allow you to destroy this family.”

“I don’t care about the Antonious.” The family was simply an obstacle to her goal. She had to play nice with them if she wanted even a tenuous bond with her father.

Stergios set his hands on his lean hips. “You need to leave and never return.”

Jodie regretted saying anything to Stergios. He could prevent her from getting what she wanted. She wished she had planned a better strategy to meet with her father. She had been too impulsive, too impatient and too scared of getting rejected again. But she couldn’t show her uncertainty or Stergios would use it against her. She lifted her chin and met his gaze. “That is out of your control.”

His smile chilled her to the bone. “It’s foolish of you to think that.”

Dread trickled down Jodie’s spine. It was foolish for her to go toe to toe with Stergios. He was a dangerous animal who lashed out if he felt threatened or cornered. "I have every right to be here."

"And I have a right—a duty—to protect my family at all cost."

She'd always known that. It was one of his traits she had admired and it used to hurt that his protection hadn't included her. "According to Dimos, I am family."

Stergios's eyes narrowed into slits. "I have *never* considered you family."

Those words would have slayed her when she was fifteen but now they slid right off her. "It's easier for you to think that, isn't it?" Jodie leaned closer, refusing to show how his words, his presence, had shaken her. "Helps you sleep better at night."

The mask fell away and exposed Stergios's wrath. A ruddy color seeped beneath his golden skin. His eyes glittered as he hunched his shoulders, ready to pounce. Jodie's chest seized as she watched his upper lip curl, pulling tightly at his scar.

"After all—" her voice trembled "—the great and virtuous Stergios Antoniou is supposed to be trustworthy and do what is right. He strives for excellence and discipline. Why, he would never have sex with a virgin without marrying her."

His jaw clenched and she knew his restraint was slipping. She had just made her most dangerous enemy very angry. She knew she should retreat and hide—no, she should beg for mercy, but the words kept spilling from her mouth.

"He would never have sex with his eighteen-year-old stepsister, right? And then walk away without a backward glance." The rejection had swamped her that night but she didn't stumble over the words now. "Discard her and throw her to the wolves."

She saw the pure hate glowing from his eyes and she wanted to recoil. Did he hate her for reminding him of his moment of weakness? Or was it something more? Did he hate her because she continued to show him what kind of man he truly was?

"But I know the real Stergios Antoniou," she confessed, driven to finish what she'd started. "I saw it that night four years ago. You're like every other man I've met. Threaten me all you want, stepbrother dear, but I'll take my chances."

CHAPTER TWO

"JODIE, WOULD YOU care for some more coffee?" Mairi Antoniou asked.

"No, thank you," she replied as she studied her father and stepmother from across the breakfast table. What should have been an intimate meal was more of a grueling interview. She had been prepared for that. Jodie wished she could spend some time with her father in private but getting him alone was proving difficult.

She was, however, making progress. Jodie couldn't believe she was back in the Antoniou family home. She'd never considered it a possibility. Yet, two days after she had been invited to Dimos's housewarming party, she was eating a late breakfast with her father and stepmother while a maid was unpacking her suitcases.

She should be celebrating. Relieved that the reunion with her father was going this smoothly, this quickly. Her instincts told her not to trust it and Jodie tried to ignore the negative voice in her head.

Looking around the breakfast room, Jodie noticed it was still fussy and formal. She always found the ivory chairs uncomfortable and the large white floral arrangements overwhelming. She studied one of the many portraits of Mairi's ancestors that covered the sea-foam-green walls. Once again, she decided that Stergios did not get his stunning masculine beauty from his mother's side.

Jodie's gaze rested on a portrait of her stepmother. She wondered what it would be like to be surrounded by family and tradition. Some of the younger Antoniou generation found the family customs constricting but she would have found comfort and privilege in continuing traditions.

Jodie looked down at her gold-rimmed china plate that had been passed down from generation to generation. Only a guest unfamiliar with the Antoniou household would think the breakfast had been planned as a feast to celebrate the return of the prodigal stepdaughter. But the family always had pastries, olives, cheese and *tiganites* in the morning. The small pancakes had been her favorite and she would often drown them with grape molasses, much to her stepmother's horror. Today she avoided the *tiganites* and had been the epitome of good behavior.

"I hope you will find your room satisfactory," Mairi said.

"Thank you." It was the same room she had stayed in years ago. In the corner on a separate floor from the rest of the family. But that didn't matter. She was going to accept what was offered and pass every test they gave. She would win the approval and love of her only living relative.

"What are your plans for today?" her father asked as he set down his paper and rose from his chair.

"I need to find a wedding present for Dimos and Zoi." It had to be appropriate but impersonal. She didn't want her gift to cause any speculation or a lecture from Stergios. Jodie winced. She wasn't going to allow her stepbrother to influence her in any way.

"And perhaps some clothes for the wedding?" Mairi suggested as she gave a pointed glance to Jodie's bright green dress. "It will be very…conservative."

Jodie nodded. Mairi had shown remarkable restraint not commenting on her short hem or towering heels. What was considered understated in New York City was different than her stepmother's opinions. She had to make some adjustments. "I understand."

"I'm sorry we have to leave just when you've arrived," Mairi said as Gregory helped her out of her chair, "but your father and I have some business to attend to in the city."

"Please don't feel like you need to entertain me." She didn't want to be the center of attention. She wanted to show her father that she could seamlessly be part of his life without any trouble or work.

"Make yourself at home," her father said as he gave an awkward pat on her shoulder before he trailed after Mairi.

Home. She grimaced as she felt a pang in her chest. This stately mansion had never been her home. She had arrived here the first time when she was fifteen after she had been kicked out of another boarding school. Jodie had felt as if she'd been on probation the moment she had first entered the vestibule. But it hadn't mattered if she had behaved or caused trouble. She was always going to be sent away to another school, another country.

Now her actions would make a difference. For better or for worse. One mistake and her father would disown her for good.

Jodie rose from her seat and strolled into the entrance hall. She barely glanced at the marble grand staircase or the carved limestone walls. It was the silence that grabbed her attention. She forgot how quiet it was in this place even though Mairi liked having her extended family live under one roof.

She linked her hands behind her back and walked outside onto the shadowy portico. Her eyes widened with pleasure as she surveyed the bold colors of the grounds, the scent of the exotic flowers and the sounds of a gurgling fountain in the distance. She sighed as the tension ebbed from her shoulders. It felt as if she had paradise all to herself.

Jodie remembered spending many hours following the web of gravel paths to escape the house. She had frequently skinny-dipped in the large lake until her stepmother found out and put a stop to it. She also climbed the trees in the wooded area, daring to go as high as she could, often ignoring Stergios's exasperation and words of warning.

Jodie descended the terrace and noticed the garden had thrived in her absence. It took her several moments to recognize the changes in the landscaping. She suspected they were made in favor of the high-tech security features. Mairi could have hidden the cameras and emergency call buttons but the Antonious always needed to see what protective measures were being taken around them.

She left the terrace and wondered if there was a new piece of sculpture or work of art. Walking past the formal flower garden, she remembered how exploring the grounds had been one of her many solitary diversions.

When she had first moved here, she'd thought having many relatives would be a blessing. For an only child who had lived in boarding schools since she was six years old, the idea of a big family was as tantalizing as it was foreign. It had ultimately been a disappointment. It wasn't easy being an outsider in a close-knit family.

It was only after Jodie had been banished that she'd realized the Antoniou home was more than a showpiece. She paused and brushed her fingertips against the velvety petals of a flower. The house and the grounds were part of the family's fortress. Mairi only felt safe when she was at home and surrounded by loved ones.

The Antonious didn't trust any outsider with the exception of Gregory. Jodie understood why. They had placed their trust in one of their own and paid the cost. They may never recover from being blindsided decades ago when Stergios was kidnapped as a child.

Jodie closed her eyes as the wave of sympathy washed over her. She had only collected bits and pieces of the story since everyone seemed to follow a pact of not discussing it. She knew Mairi and her ex-husband had been in an ugly custody dispute and that Stergios's father had hired a team to kidnap his son. Stergios had only been seven years old.

Jodie blinked away the sting of unshed tears as she imagined a young and vulnerable Stergios. Mairi was a tigress when it came to her only child but she didn't find him until he was nine. Stergios had lived on the run and in horrible conditions. He had emerged scarred, malnourished and tormented from the experience.

From the day Stergios had been taken, the house and grounds became impenetrable. So had the Antoniou family. Jodie accepted the fact and she knew their wariness wasn't entirely personal.

Jodie sighed and slowly retraced her steps, returning to the portico. She saw a flash of movement in the corner of her eye and turned to see Stergios. He emerged from the wooded area, the gravel crunching under his running shoes as he jogged toward the house with a punishing pace. The fight-or-flight response swirled in her chest. She cast a quick glance in the direction of the formal garden, her heart skipping a beat as her hands bunched into fists.

It was too late to disappear, Jodie decided as she watched Stergios get closer. She tried not to notice that he only wore a dark pair of running shorts, or the way his golden skin glistened. Her gaze darted to his broad shoulders and then to his muscular arms. Jodie felt a spurt of heat low in her belly and she wasn't sure where to look. She focused on his chest and followed the path of his dark hair. Her attention rested on his V-cut abs.

He didn't break his rhythm as he jogged onto the terrace and then stepped onto the portico. He passed her as if he wasn't going to acknowledge her presence.

"I didn't know you were still living here," she blurted out.

Stergios stopped without turning around. "I don't." Sweat ran down his spine but he didn't sound out of breath. He placed his hands on his lean hips and stretched. She was mesmerized by the play of muscles and the faint crisscross of scars that ran down his back. "I have a home of my own but I stay here when I'm in Athens."

Jodie stepped in front of him, blocking his way. It was irritating that he wouldn't deign to look at her. She inhaled his scent and went still. It was hot, sweaty and male. A blush crept up her neck and into her face. She didn't know why it left her flustered.

"How long are you planning to stay?" Jodie asked. His nearness was almost her undoing. Her breasts felt heavy and tight and she crossed her arms against her chest.

"For as long as you are, *pethi mou*," he said. "I'm only here to keep an eye on you."

"What?" Jodie's lips parted as a thought occurred to her. "Is that why I was invited to the family home? To make surveillance more convenient for you?"

His eyes glittered with amusement. "It was thoughtful of you to accept."

Jodie abruptly looked away and stared at the door that led to the house. She should have known it hadn't been her father's idea. Her intuition had been correct. She shouldn't trust this act of hospitality.

She wasn't going to let this get her down. Jodie clenched her teeth as she encouraged the flicker of determination to catch fire. It didn't matter why she was invited. She was here and she was going to make the most of it.

"Going to go pack?" he asked in a drawl.

Her arms tightened around her as if she was holding herself together. "Why would I?" she asked as she slowly met his gaze. "I'm getting what I want."

"Are you sure? Dimos doesn't live here."

"Wonderful," she declared. "Now you don't

have follow him like a guard dog and save him from predatory women. That must free up so much time for you."

There was a heavy beat of silence. "That wasn't the only reason I stopped Dimos."

"Of course it was. If Dimos had sex with me, a woman supposedly under the protection of the Antoniou family, he would have been stuck marrying me instead of the heiress of your choice." She paused, not sure if she should say anything more. "Do you even know why we were down in the wine cellar that night? We were going to break into the good stuff while everyone was out of the house."

"It didn't look that way when I tore you two apart."

Jodie glared at him. When Stergios had intervened, Dimos had her in a tight hold and had been sticking his tongue down her throat. She hadn't been trying to get closer to Dimos—she had been pushing him away! "I was never interested in him. There was no way we were going to have sex!"

Stergios lifted an eyebrow. "Then how do you explain what happened between us?"

She felt her face turn bright red. It had been different with Stergios. When Jodie had returned from her last finishing school fiasco, she had become violently aware of her stepbrother's sexual allure. It didn't matter that he was eight years older or that he was too intense for someone like her.

But Jodie didn't want anyone to notice how much power Stergios had over her. She had some pride! The man hated her and yet she wanted to get closer to him. She had become an expert at hiding her attraction. Or so she thought. Now she knew why she'd always bickered with Stergios. Why they'd always seemed to get under each other's skin.

When Stergios had shoved Dimos up the stairs that night, she had launched into an argument with her stepbrother that felt as though it had been simmering for weeks. Vicious words had been exchanged and nothing had been held back.

To this day Jodie wasn't sure what had happened next. What had been the trigger? Had she made the first move or had he? All she knew was that her mouth had slammed against his. His kiss, his touch, had set her free. It was as if they had exploded out of their cages. She'd clawed and bit as he ruthlessly made his claim. She'd encouraged him to give her everything he had. Their coupling had been fast and feral.

She hadn't experienced anything like it since. Even now her heart pumped hard and her skin felt scorched as she remembered the way he took her against the wall.

"I looked for you after that night," Stergios confessed.

She jerked back as the memories splintered. "No, you didn't," she said softly. "You left like a bat out of hell. Where did you go?"

He speared his hands in his long hair and gave a guttural sigh. "It doesn't matter."

It had mattered to her. She had felt rejected and abandoned. Used.

"You'd left Greece by the time I returned," Stergios said, staring blindly at the garden. "I went to America to find you. I assumed you went to your mother's but you had already left by the time I arrived in New York. Your mother wasn't helpful in how to contact you."

She gave an awkward nod. Carla Little had not been a motherly, nurturing kind of woman who needed to know what her daughter was doing. "Mom was in the middle of a business deal that would have determined her legacy," she mumbled. "She couldn't afford any distraction."

"I kept looking for you," he admitted with great reluctance before he returned his piercing gaze on her. "No one seemed to know where you were."

Her parents hadn't been interested in finding out. While her friends were envious of her independence, the lack of parental concern had always embarrassed Jodie. "I knew how to take care of myself," she said. "Why was it so urgent to find me?"

"I wanted to check on you."

Jodie drew her head back. She wasn't sure what to say. Of all the people who had been part of that night, he had been the only one who tried to contact her. Even though he had made it clear how much he didn't like her, how little she meant to him.

Stergios watched her with an intensity that pinned her to the spot. "You were a virgin and I was…rough."

Jodie frowned when she saw his stony expression. Stergios had been beating himself up about that night when she'd savored the primal and naked responses. It had been everything she had hoped for with the man who had starred in her secret fantasies.

And why did he have to bring up her inexperience? Her eyes widened with surprise. "Wait… were you going to insist on *marriage*?" she asked. She knew how the Antoniou males thought. They had very old-fashioned views. The men married the virgins and had affairs with experienced women.

"I didn't use protection that night," he said stiffly, as if the oversight went against his personal code of honor. "I needed to know if there were consequences."

Oh. He wasn't worried about her as much as he was concerned about an illegitimate child. Disappointment crashed through her. She wanted to hunch her shoulders and curl into herself as if she could contain the pain. "There weren't," she said in a whisper.

Stergios gave a sharp nod. "I knew I had to seek you out because you wouldn't have volunteered that information with me."

Not necessarily. He always assumed the worst

in her. “If you thought that, why did you give up looking for me? We’re talking about your child, the Antoniou heir,” she said grandly as she spread her hands up high in the air. “You would have searched the world if you thought that was a possibility.”

“I stopped looking a few months later.” His features hardened as he gave her an unforgiving look. “There was a picture of you online and you were definitely not pregnant.”

She frowned. “What picture?”

Stergios sneered from the memory. “You were on a yacht in the Caribbean with that royal playboy.” He spat out the last word as if it was a curse.

Jodie wanted to cringe. The prince had been a mistake. She had been looking for love. She had been desperate to *be* loved and found a playboy instead. Unfortunately, she had found a few playboys on her search for love before she wised up.

“I see,” she said calmly as she watched Stergios’s lip curl with disgust. “And suddenly it no longer mattered that I was a virgin or eighteen.”

He shrugged. “I might have been your first, but then you threw yourself at the next man who showed any interest," he declared as he turned away. "You were no longer my problem."

No longer my problem. The words echoed in her mind as she dazedly watched Stergios stride into the house. Once he'd decided that she "belonged" to another man, she had no longer existed.

Jodie hissed air between her clenched teeth as the pain ricocheted. He had ruthlessly cleaved her out of his life. He had moved on without missing a step. It was a fear she struggled with constantly. The fear of becoming invisible. Forgotten.

But she had no idea it was that easy.

She needed to work harder to become unforgettable to those who mattered. It was an impossible task, Jodie decided as she took the steps back to the garden, intent on getting away from the house, from Stergios. As she marched along the path she gradually realized what she had to do. She was going to use her wealth to become an indispensible member of the family. She might be unlovable now, but money could change anything.

CHAPTER THREE

HE HAD UNDERESTIMATED JODIE, Stergios decided later that night. He considered what he had seen at the family dinner a few moments ago and scowled. Not only had she gained her father's attention with the mention of an expensive gift for his upcoming birthday, but Jodie had also excelled in the area that had consistently been her downfall. She had been the quintessential dinner companion, delighting the surliest of his uncles and making fast friends with the younger wives and fiancées.

Stergios reluctantly admired Jodie's strategy. She had approached the outer circle of his family and was slowly gaining allies. He couldn't have this.

He leaned against the marble newel post as he watched Jodie descend the staircase like a regal queen. She had reapplied her bright red lipstick after dinner and he found it difficult to look away from her mouth. He couldn't fault her long-sleeved black dress. It should have been modest but it clung lovingly to her thighs. The white stripe zigzagging from her shoulder to her waist and hips was pure Jodie. Despite her attempts to blend in with the crowd she couldn't wear anything that might have her fade into the background.

"You gave a worthy performance at dinner tonight," he said as she drew closer.

She cast him a haughty look. "I don't know what you're talking about."

"You were very proper." He should have appreciated the charade. Stergios remembered the family dinners she'd attended in the past. At times he hadn't known if she'd been intentionally provocative or if she'd been unable to control her tongue. "You're playing it safe. That's not like you."

She stood on the last step and met his gaze. "I know what is expected of me."

"Especially if a wrong move will harm your chances with this family." She wasn't going to make a mistake soon. Jodie was using all of her knowledge from her past visits to dazzle and deceive. "What is it you want from us? Status? A favor?"

"As I have said before, I no longer want to be estranged from my father."

She was sticking to that story but Stergios knew there had to be something more. What had happened that would cause this change of heart? What did her father have that she wanted? "Why?"

She frowned. "He's my father."

"He's also the one who threw you out of this home." And to someone like Jodie, that act would have been unforgiveable.

The corner of her mouth dipped before she looked away. "Emotions ran high that night," she said quietly. "We said and did things we later regretted. It's time to forgive and move on."

Stergios raised an eyebrow at her practiced answer. "You think Gregory regretted his actions? That he wants forgiveness?"

She hesitated and glanced at the music room where her father was chatting with guests. "I can only speak for myself," she replied in a faraway voice.

"You didn't think the timing of that night had

been suspicious?" He crossed his arms as he watched her closely. "He cast you out of his life when you were eighteen."

Jodie's head jerked and she gave him a cold stare. "Mairi kicked me out," she corrected him. "This is her house and my father was obligated to agree with her."

"And Gregory was no longer receiving child support from your mother." His quiet tone didn't soften the blow.

She pressed her lips before she spoke. "You think my father only tolerated me because of the money?"

There were many times when he had believed that. Gregory may have won full custody of Jodie, but he had constantly sent her overseas to any school that would take her. When she was away, it was as if Gregory forgot her existence. Each time Jodie had been expelled from a school and came here to live, Gregory had made it clear that the living arrangements would be temporary.

"He didn't get rid of me the moment he could. I hadn't just turned eighteen," she reminded him. "If that had been his reason, he would have kicked me out months before."

Stergios knew he had wounded her. Her rigid stance and cool tone didn't give her away. It was in the way she tried to give a scornful smile. Her tremulous lips ruined the effect.

He had dug in and exposed a fear that had settled deep in her heart. It gave him no pleasure. But Stergios knew he couldn't hold back if he wanted her to leave. He had to go in for the kill.

"It's common knowledge that Gregory wanted to become a father so he could eventually live off the child support."

Her forced smile tightened. "Yes, I've heard what was said during the divorce proceedings. That was one lawyer's argument and it doesn't make it true." She took the last step and headed for the music room to join the others.

"Why would you want a relationship with a man who only showed an interest in you for the money?" he called after her.

"Perhaps you should ask your mother that question." She whirled around. There was restrained anger in her movement but her expression was coldly polite. "My father married Mairi for money. She married him because he's a respectable escort. He's not a danger to her fortune or family like your father was."

Stergios's head snapped back. No one discussed Elias Pagonis in this house. In front of him. *No one.* Stergios had shed his father's name years ago but he couldn't rid himself of the memories and the damage Pagonis had created.

Jodie took a step closer as if she wasn't aware of the emotional grenade she'd just lobbed. "Mairi and my father have been married for ten years and they have grown fond of each other. Is it really outside the realm of possibility that my father can grow to love his only child?"

Stergios struggled to focus as old anger swelled inside him. He wouldn't allow Jodie to distract him with the mention of Pagonis. "Are you going to buy Gregory's love with your inheritance and hope it becomes the real thing one day?"

"Do you think that's the only way I can get love? By paying for it?"

Stergios heard the crack in her voice and the weak sound pulled at him. "Be careful with this plan," he said roughly as he fought for control over his emotions. "You'll soon run out of money.

And when that happens, Gregory will have no use for you."

"Why are you giving me advice, Stergios? I can't believe it's from the goodness of your black, withered heart. If my father loses interest in me, that will suit your purposes."

"Because I don't believe that's why you're here." Rejection was the one thing Jodie Little couldn't excuse. "You can't accept that Gregory got rid of you."

"He didn't get rid of me." She leaned forward and he noticed the suspicious moisture in her blue eyes. "He had to make a choice between his wife and his daughter."

"And he'll make the same choice over and over again." Stergios almost missed the flicker of pain before she blinked. "You have money now but it's nothing compared to what we have. We have more money, influence and power. You can't compete."

"I'm not trying to take him away from your mother." Her voice was rough with annoyance.

"*Oxi*, it's worse. You're trying to become part of this family." He viewed her plan as an invasion and he would use all of his resources to prevent that. "Do you actually believe we're going to lower our guard and let you in?"

"No, of course not. It didn't happen before. Why should it now?" She shook her head as if she was suddenly weary. "I am not the enemy, Stergios. I don't have the power to hurt anyone."

Stergios wanted to scoff at that declaration. "I disagree. I've seen the damage you cause without even trying."

Jodie set her mouth into a grim line. "Don't put all the blame on me."

"You have always been trouble." He raked his hand through his hair. "If you weren't causing me headaches, you were destroying everything important to me. I can't have you anywhere near Dimos's wedding."

Jodie stared at him silently for a moment before she raised her chin. "Sorry to hear nothing is going your way, Stergios," she said with a dismissive wave of her hand. "You better get used to it while I'm around."

The woman didn't understand, Stergios decided. His gaze rested on the sway of her hips as she strutted to the music room. Jodie assumed he played fair but when it came to protecting his family, he wasn't constrained by a gentleman's code of conduct. He had learned early in life what it took to fight to the death. He followed the law of the jungle and always won. Always.

Stergios wandered into the music room a few minutes later. It had taken some time to purge the thought of Pagonis and rein in his emotions. Jodie had hit her mark and it appeared she had done so without any strategy. It was as though she could see through him however much he tried to dissemble.

He stood by the door as he watched one of the guests, yet another heiress and family friend, play his mother's favorite sonata on the piano. Everyone seemed spellbound by the display of technical precision but the music didn't reach him. Rarely did anything pierce through his armor these days. Just Jodie Little. Stergios frowned at that troubling thought.

"Stergios?" He turned and saw Zoi Volakis. He wasn't sure how long she had been standing there. She was a petite woman with dramatic features who dressed just like every other female in his social circle. "I've been meaning to ask. What exactly is Jodie to this family?"

"She is Gregory's daughter from his first marriage," Stergios answered. He refused to say she was part of the family. Legally she was a relative but her actions proved otherwise. She wouldn't think twice about destroying his family.

"She doesn't look anything like him," Zoi decided. "And they act like strangers."

So he wasn't the only one who noticed that. "They're Americans. New Yorkers."

She gave a wry chuckle. "That must explain it. How long does Jodie plan to stay?"

Her casual tone hit a wrong note and Stergios went on alert. "She hasn't said. Why?"

Zoi hesitated, as if she was reluctant to say anything. "Jodie is very close to Dimos."

He looked around the music room for his cousin. Frustration and something dark and dangerous bloomed inside him when he saw Dimos and Jodie standing by the windows, apart from the other guests. "They grew up as cousins in the same house."

Stergios recognized Dimos's awestruck look. He had seen that expression on his cousin's face in a picture four years ago. Mairi had sent him a picture of a family event when he had been working on an assignment overseas. It was more than infatuation. He had known at that moment that Dimos wanted to claim Jodie.

And Stergios returned home immediately after seeing that picture. He had done everything in his power to keep Dimos and Jodie from getting together. Stergios could tell himself it was to protect the merger but there had been darker, more primal reasons he hadn't wanted to explore.

"Is there anything I should know?" Zoi asked.

"No, of course not," Stergios replied smoothly. "Dimos wants to marry you."

She nodded her head but she didn't appear relieved by his answer. "Dimos and I do not have a love match, but I take this commitment seriously," Zoi said. "I'm getting married because it's my duty to my family."

Stergios tensed when he heard the warning underneath Zoi's polite tone. He didn't need this. Not now. "Dimos knows how important this merger is for both our families."

"Good, but I am not as self-sacrificing as you may think." She cast another glance in Dimos's direction before she lifted her chin with injured pride. "I had tolerated the delays and setbacks before we got engaged, but I will not be humiliated by my husband's wandering eye."

Stergios gritted his teeth as he watched Zoi walk out of the music room. They were so close to getting this merger settled but it could all fall apart in the next few days. He took part of the blame. He had pushed Jodie too far and had hurt her feelings. She retaliated the only way she knew how.

He strode toward his cousin and Jodie. They seemed to be in a world of their own with their heads tilted close to each other. Dimos must have caught a glimpse of him. His forehead was creased with worry as he cautiously approached Stergios. "What's wrong?"

"Stay away from Jodie," he warned in a low, fierce tone.

Dimos flushed as he glowered at him. "Why? You can hate her all you want but—"

"She isn't going to share her body or her bed with you." Stergios watched with satisfaction as Jodie slipped out of the music room and hurried to the grand staircase. She wouldn't be a concern for the rest of the night.

His cousin continued to splutter with outrage. "What the—"

"She's leading you on because I told her not to," Stergios said with brutal honesty. "Haven't you learned anything about this woman?"

"You have no—"

Stergios leaned forward and watched with satisfaction as his cousin took a cautious step back. "And if this wedding doesn't happen, if you try anything with Jodie, I will cut you out of this family."

Dimos's jaw went slack before his eyes glittered with hate.

"You're supposed to be engaged," he said as the anger flashed hot inside him. "Act like it. Go find your fiancée and pretend Jodie Little doesn't exist."

Stergios turned his back on his cousin and forced a genial expression before he mingled with the guests. Now if only he could afford the same luxury and act as if the threat of Jodie Little didn't loom over his family.

Just a couple more days, Jodie thought as she rested her head against the soft leather chair. It was almost over and yet the knowledge didn't relieve the coiling tension inside her. Dimos's wedding was to be held the following evening and she would have finally proven to Stergios that she had no plans of revenge or destruction. But intuition told her that he wasn't going to stop. He was going to find a way to push her out for good.

Jodie shifted in her seat and tried to relax. The ride in Stergios's private helicopter was loud but she wore a headset to communicate. She had found the all-white interior and luxurious touches more intimidating than comfortable. It was just another reminder that the Antonious had more money and power than she.

She glanced at Stergios. He sat in the chair next to her and read his tablet. He was dressed more for a funeral than a wedding in his black designer suit and black silk tie. He had been moody since they had left the house and she had done her best to ignore him.

Jodie crossed her arms and tapped the pointed toe of her black stiletto heels against the floor. "I still don't understand why I had to arrive at the wedding with you."

He didn't look up from the screen. "It's a matter of logistics."

She made a face. "You have a thousand relatives and not one could include me in their travel plans?"

"Not one."

"And it has nothing to do with the fact that you won't let me out of your sight until Dimos gets married?"

He swiped his fingers against the touch screen. "That is correct, *pethi mou*," he murmured distractedly.

He had been her shadow for the past few days and she had been unable to shake him off. It didn't matter if she talked nonstop or gave him the silent treatment. He didn't care if she wanted to have a private moment with her father or get lost in a crowded party. He had always been at her side.

Jodie pointedly looked away from him and nervously peered through the window. She didn't like the way the dark gray clouds filled the sky or how the choppy waves crashed against each other in the Aegean Sea. She hoped they landed soon before the weather got rougher.

Just as she was going to ask how much longer the trip would last, Jodie saw the island as the helicopter pilot started his descent. Her lips parted with surprise when she saw the rolling hills covered with fat, leafy trees. After meeting Zoi and her family, she had expected one big amusement park filled with pristine beaches, golf courses and all the amenities. This looked like an uninhabited island.

As the helicopter set down on the landing pad, Jodie caught a glimpse of a house. It was white and modern with clean lines and a flat roof. It wasn't a mansion and she assumed it wasn't the main residence. It probably belonged to one of the islanders.

She scrambled out of the helicopter inelegantly in her form-fitting orange dress and sky-high heels but she refused Stergios's assistance. She stood at the edge of the helipad as she watched him confer with the pilot.

"Where is your suitcase?" Jodie asked as he walked past her, effortlessly carrying her bags.

"Everything I need is here," he said, patting his briefcase.

She didn't doubt it. The man was outrageously

sexy and didn't have to primp or make any effort to look good. It really wasn't fair.

Jodie followed him along the gravel path, falling behind thanks to her spindly heels. She heard the whine of the helicopter behind her as it ascended. "It's very quiet here," she commented as she brushed her hair away from her face.

"Not for much longer, I'm sure."

There was no music or the sound of conversation. What kind of event was this going to be? A wedding should have a festive tone, even if it was arranged.

"The way Zoi had talked about her wedding, I thought there'd be more decorations," she said as she tried to walk faster. "I'm not saying she'd line the helipad with flowers but I wouldn't put it past her."

Stergios didn't say anything as he waited for her to catch up.

Jodie stopped next to him and placed her hands on her hips as she looked around. It was strange that no one had met them. "Where is everyone?"

His mouth settled into a harsh line. "At the Volakis Island, I assume."

Jodie frowned with confusion. "Wait. What?"

She shook her head as she tried to make sense of what he said. "Isn't this the Volakis Island?"

"*Oxi*, this is my home," he replied in a resigned tone.

She glanced around again at the white sand beach and leafy trees. The island was unspoiled and isolated. Free from any distraction. It suited Stergios.

"Why did we have to stop here?" She whirled around and watched the helicopter fade into the gray sky. "Why didn't you ask the pilot to wait?"

"He'll be back in three days."

"What?" Her heel skidded against the path. She grabbed his sleeve but her hand barely wrapped around his muscular arm. "I don't understand what is going on."

His eyes were cold and wintry when she met his gaze. "You didn't leave when you had a chance," he said in a clipped tone. "You didn't stay away from Dimos. You left me no choice."

Her mouth parted as the shock and confusion crashed inside her. "What are you saying?"

"You're not going to the wedding," he announced. "You're stuck here with me until I decide it's safe to let you go."

CHAPTER FOUR

"YOU CAN'T DO THAT!" She looked around the island, the scent of the briny ocean and the promise of rain suddenly overwhelming. Her head began to spin as she took deep gulps of air. "I did not agree to this. My father is expecting me at this wedding. It will embarrass him if I unexpectedly don't show up."

"You have no choice in the matter. I suggest you get inside before the storm hits."

She waved her hands in the air as she spluttered with outrage. "Do you honestly believe that I will just follow you? Only because you say so?" She reached inside her purse and grabbed her phone. "You forget that I'm not an Antoniou who mindlessly obeys your orders."

"Put that away," Stergios replied. "You're not going to reach anyone. There is no internet or phone connection on this island."

She refused to believe him. A man as important and powerful as Stergios Antoniou would have all of the latest technology. But as she held up her phone she saw he was telling the truth. Maybe she was in a bad range. Maybe she had to go higher on the island.

"People are going to worry if we don't show up." She hated how her voice escalated as she took short, choppy breaths. "Especially you. You have to be at the wedding. You've been part of it every step of the way. Will it still go on if you don't manage every moment of it?"

"One of my assistants is calling my mother to let her know we've been detained because of mechanical problems."

He sounded indifferent. She hated it. Hated him. "You thought of everything. How long have you been planning this?"

"It came to me this morning. Does it matter?" He gave a shrug before glanced at the darkening sky. "We need to go inside."

"No." She looked around wildly, her heart pumping. There had to be a boat around here. A Jet Ski. Something. She would find a way to escape if she had to comb through every inch of this island.

"Come along, *pethi mou*," he said with a bite of impatience. "The caretaker is away but you are safe with me. After all, you are my guest."

She scoffed and cast him a look of disbelief. "I am your hostage."

Stergios flinched. He went pale as his expression turned blank. "What did you say?" His voice was a rasp.

"You heard me." Jodie didn't like how the air suddenly crackled between them. Alarm trickled down her spine. "You have kidnapped me. *You*, of all people."

He dropped the suitcases on the ground as if his fingers went slack. "You don't know what you're talking about." His hand sliced through the air. "This is not a kidnapping."

"You are detaining me against my will." Her voice faded as he approached her. It took all of her courage to stand her ground.

"Did I take you by force?" he asked through clenched teeth. "Are you in chains?"

Jodie saw the haunted look in his eyes and she knew he was wrestling with old memories. But she couldn't afford to show him any sympathy.

"What are you saying? That I'm not your prisoner because I had a comfortable ride over here?"

He stabbed his finger in the direction of the house behind him. "You will have a room of your own and plenty of food. You will have comfort and privacy. I will make sure every one of your needs are met."

"As long as I do what you tell me?" She flung her hands high in the air. "Forget it. I'm not going into that house. How do I know that you won't lock me in the room?"

"There are no bars on the windows. You can come and go as you please."

"As long as I stay on the island," Jodie added. "That still makes me a prisoner."

He closed his eyes and drew in air between his teeth. His hands clenched and unclenched at his side. "This is not a kidnapping."

She crossed her arms and glared at him. "Then get me off this island right now."

He paused as the tension radiated from his body. Just when she thought Stergios was going to explode, he opened his eyes and took a step back. "*Oxi*. No."

His answer was so quiet and calm. He didn't

care what he did or to whom. "I should have expected this." She shook her head in disgust. "This is why you intimidate everyone. They can sense that you aren't the gentleman you pretend to be. They know there's a wild animal just underneath ready to pounce."

"I'm going inside." Stergios walked away and grabbed the luggage. "You can do whatever you please."

She stamped her foot as the fury ripped through her. "What have I done to deserve this?" she called out to him. "Why do you hate me so much?"

Stergios slowly turned around. His eyes were cold and his mouth was curved in a stern frown. She couldn't tell what he was thinking or feeling. He was back in control. "Hate you?" he asked. "Jodie, I don't give a damn about you."

"You're lying," she yelled. "You wish you could forget me. You hate how I make you feel."

The corner of his mouth hitched. "Dream on."

"I could tell that night in the wine cellar," she blurted out. "That's why you ran away. You were ashamed that I had that much power over you."

Ashamed that, of all women, it had been me.

Stergios's harsh features tightened as he hunched his shoulders. She could tell she struck a nerve. He was trying to hold himself back before he retaliated.

Jodie pressed her fingertips against her lips. She had to curb her tongue. She was already vulnerable to this man. She didn't need Stergios to figure out how he made her feel. She was the one who lost control when they were together. He was the one who had power over her.

"I'm going to make you regret this," Jodie said in a hiss as she turned around and went back up the steps. "And you will have no one to blame but yourself."

Stergios paced along the windows that overlooked the beach. He had discarded his jacket hours ago and had rolled up the sleeves of his white shirt. It was turning dark and the rain was still coming down hard. Jodie had not made an attempt to find shelter.

He paused and looked for a flash of the bright orange designer dress. He had seen the pop of color every once in a while as she searched the island for an escape. Stergios now spotted her sitting on the wet sand near the house. Her blond hair was plastered against her head and her soaked dress clung to her body as the ocean waves lapped against her bare feet. With her slumped shoulders and outstretched legs, she appeared weary. Defeated.

Kidnapped.

Stergios hissed and rubbed his hands over his face. Jodie always knew what to say to pierce his armor. She would do anything to get a reaction. But it wasn't going to work. This was not a kidnapping.

He knew what a kidnapping felt like. It was a constant state of fear and of not knowing. It was howling pain punctuated with numbness. At times he hadn't felt human. He had been a pawn, a package. His childhood, his innocence, had been stripped from him in an instant. Worst of all, he had discovered what he was capable of and how far he would go to find freedom.

He understood what it felt like to be taken. And still… Stergios stared at Jodie. He replayed his actions in his mind and it had been strangely familiar. The truth suddenly cracked his resistance wide open. It was as if jagged shards dug deep in his chest and he couldn't breathe.

He had made the same decision his father had made years ago.

Stergios took a shallow breath as the pain scored through him. This hadn't been a delay or a detour. He had kidnapped someone. He had followed his instincts and had snatched Jodie in broad daylight.

He rested his forehead against the windowpane and struggled to remain standing as a cold sweat prickled his skin. The idea to abduct Jodie had come naturally and he hadn't questioned it.

Stergios closed his eyes as the nausea swept through him. After all these years of fighting the possibility, blood will out. He thought he had been protecting his family by keeping Jodie away. Instead, he had uncovered one of his deepest fears. He had always pushed himself to be a better man than his father. To distance himself from everything the man had represented.

But every time he looked in the mirror, he was reminded of his father. Despite his achievements and milestones, nothing could cover up the fact that he was Elias Pagonis's son.

Stergios stepped away from the window. He thrust his hands in his hair, but he didn't feel the sting of his fingers dragging along his scalp. He had to fix this. Redeem himself. Find a way to erase his actions.

He glanced up at the sky and noticed how the trees swayed against the wind. There was no way they could leave the island tonight in this weather. And could he allow Jodie to attend the wedding? Was he willing to take that risk?

Stergios would consider the consequences later. Right now she was his obligation. He couldn't let anything happen to her while she was here.

He strode out of the house, the door banging against the wall, and marched through the sand. Jodie's eyes widened as she caught a glimpse of him. She scooped up her shoes as she struggled to stand up.

"You are so stubborn," he called out over the roar of the storm.

She scurried back, poised to run. "Don't talk to me! I'm furious with you."

"Are you going to stay out here all night?" The wind whipped his hair as the cold sheet of rain stung his bare skin.

"Yes," she spat out. "I'd rather catch pneumonia than be your prisoner."

"You always pick the wrong choice," he said in a growl as he rubbed the water from his eyes. "Instead of showing common sense, you have to make some dramatic statement."

"This from a man who thought kidnapping was the only option."

He had had enough. Stergios lunged forward and grabbed Jodie. She screamed as he gathered her in his arms. She fought for her release, kicking and slapping, demanding that he set her down.

"Keep that up and I'll drop you," he warned as he walked across the beach.

"Try it and I'll take you down with me."

He entered the house and walked through the living area, past the welcoming heat of the fire he had built in the fireplace. "There are two bedrooms," he told her as he approached the door. "Mine is on the other side of the house. This one is yours. You can stay here for as long as you like."

"I bet you'd like that," Jodie said as she kicked wildly in the air. "You want me to hide in here.

Stay out of the way so you can forget what you've done."

He was finished with dramatic, impertinent women who brought nothing but disruption into his life. All he wanted was peace. A sense of security. Anything that blunted the tension inside him.

Stergios carefully set Jodie onto the floor. "Your bathroom is through there," he said, nodding in the direction of one of the doors. "Your suitcase is in the closet."

"That's it?" She stood before him barefoot and in a sodden dress, but she didn't appear small or vulnerable. "That's all you have to say to me?"

He wiped the dripping water from his forehead with the back of his hand. "You do not want to know what is going through my mind right now."

"Bringing me here was a mistake," she said with a snarl. "You assumed I was a threat to the Antoniou-Volakis marriage and you thought you were so clever to keep me away. But the truth is I'm a threat to you. I'm the only person who's cracked you. I see you—the real you."

"You're not so special," he said as he stepped over the threshold. "You're the only one who has yet to realize that you should be afraid of the real me." He quietly closed the door behind him and strode away.

An hour later, Jodie wrenched open her bedroom door and entered the main room of the house. She could have stayed in the hot shower all night but the last thing she would do was hide in her room. As much as she wanted to avoid Stergios, she wasn't going make herself invisible.

She tightened the belt around her robe, wishing she had something heavier than the ivory silk one that didn't reach her knees. With any luck, Stergios would be in his room.

Jodie took a moment to look around. It wasn't a surprise that Stergios's island getaway was light, airy and luxurious. He had always surrounded himself with exquisite beauty.

There were large windows that offered a panoramic view of the ocean. The cathedral ceiling's exposed rafters and the stone floors seemed to reflect the island environment. The modern fireplace in the center of the main room was a showpiece. She was tempted to curl up on one of the white couches and get warmed by the dying fire.

Jodie pressed her hand against her growling stomach and decided she needed to get something to eat first. She went in search for the kitchen and found that the large room was casual and inviting. Jodie skidded to a stop when she saw Stergios sitting at the kitchen table.

Her heart banged hard against her chest when she saw him sprawled on a heavy wood chair. Stergios had discarded his business suit for a long-sleeve blue T-shirt and faded jeans. His large feet were bare and his damp hair was slicked back.

There was a clear liquor bottle and a shot glass resting by his hand. She caught a scent of the strong alcohol and suspected it was Tsipouro. Only Stergios would take a drink made for social gatherings and treat it as a solitary event.

Stergios didn't glance up. "Go away, Jodie."

She jerked, unaware that he had seen her. Jodie grabbed the collar of her robe closer as she fought for courage. "I wish I could, but my movements are extremely limited."

He lifted his head and silently glared at her.

"Anyway, I'm hungry," she announced as she padded barefoot to the large refrigerator. "Do you have anything for the prisoner? Maybe some bread and water?"

"Go back to your room," he said as he returned his attention to his shot glass. "I am not in the mood for company."

Jodie closed the refrigerator door and studied him. She hadn't seen him in this kind of mood. It was stormy and unpredictable. "Then just ignore me. You're a pro at it."

He gave a huff of a laugh and slumped against his chair. "You refuse to be ignored. You know how to get attention. You can't help it."

"I don't like being invisible," she admitted.

"I could never accuse you of that." He poured another shot and held it out for her.

She crossed her arms and leaned against the kitchen counter. "No, thanks. I don't drink."

"Liar," he said huskily. "It was one of the top three reasons you got kicked out of school. Boys, alcohol and cheating. And didn't you say you snuck into the wine cellar with Dimos to find alcohol?"

"Reason enough to give it up, don't you think?"

He gave her a mocking salute with the shot

glass. Downing it one gulp, he set the glass down with a thud.

"I've never seen you like this, Stergios," she murmured. He often moved with fluid grace. Tonight he seemed uncoordinated. "Are you drunk?"

"I'm working on it." He pushed the shot glass away as he grimaced. There was a beat of tense silence before he spoke again. "You were right about me. I am my father's son."

"I didn't say that," Jodie insisted. She didn't know much about Elias Pagonis but she knew his actions had been reprehensible.

"You didn't have to. I…kidnapped you," he said with an odd hitch in his voice. "I can't remove all traces of my actions but I will make it right. A helicopter will be here first thing in the morning and it'll take you to the wedding. I will remain here."

She stared at him. There had to be a catch. Why was he allowing her to attend the wedding? Stergios Antoniou never admitted defeat.

He dragged his gaze to meet hers. His dark eyes were troubled and filled with remorse. "I'm sorry that I frightened you."

Jodie drew her head back at the surprising apology. "You don't make me scared. You make me angry," she clarified.

He gave a harsh bark of laughter. "Typical. You don't even know when to be worried. I should warn you that I'm in a very dangerous mood."

"Stergios..." she said as she approached him.

"You know what I'm capable of when I'm sober." Stergios rubbed his hand against the dark stubble on his jaw. "You should go hide in your room."

Jodie ignored the trepidation curling deep in her belly. "No, you can't just send me away and act like I don't exist."

"You don't understand." His voice was strained. "I am feeling volatile."

"You usually do when I'm around."

He went still and gave her a sidelong look. "Careful, *pethi mou*."

"And you carry around this guilt about what happened between us in the wine cellar. Why? I take equal responsibility for that."

"You feel guilty, too," he decided. "Guilty for going too far. For surrendering to me."

She felt her skin heat as she remembered the

glorious moment she had yielded to him. "I don't feel guilty."

"Then why did you lie?" He sat up straight in his chair. "That's what I can't figure out. Why did you tell everyone that we didn't have sex that night?"

"No one would have believed me." It wasn't the full truth but it was a reason Stergios could accept. "Your family acts like you are a god who can do no wrong. They treated me like I was a plague that kept returning."

He shook his head. "You lied because you were ashamed."

"No, I wasn't. I'm not." She had been fascinated with Stergios. She had been infatuated him with the wild abandon of someone who had never felt that way before. The only thing she was ashamed about was how much he meant to her when she meant nothing to him.

"You could have saved yourself that night," Stergios said. "If you had told them that I had taken advantage of you then—"

"Taken advantage? I was with you every step of the way." Her voice rose. "Why would I make that kind of accusation? I don't want anyone to think that about you. That's why I stuck by my story. I lied to protect you."

He leaned forward, resting his arms against his legs. "Protect me?" His voice flicked like the tip of a whip.

"I could tell that you were ashamed of what happened that night. You hated yourself because of it. Why would I advertise that?"

"I don't need your protection," he said in a withering tone as he stood. "You are the one who needs protection from me."

"No, I don't."

"I had lost control that night, but so did you," Stergios said in a low, gravelly voice as he approached her. "I had unleashed something wild. I felt it when I was deep inside you."

She tried to appear unaffected by his statement but she couldn't hide her reaction. The way her pulse fluttered at the base of her throat. The kick of lust that made her gasp. The delicious heaviness that settled in her pelvis.

"And I can do it again." His voice was thick as his hooded eyes focused on her mouth. "One touch and you will come apart."

Jodie's lips stung with awareness. "You killed

anything I felt for you when you walked away that night."

"Which just makes it worse, doesn't it?" He rested his big hands on the kitchen counter, trapping her. "You don't want to desire me," he said in a mesmerizing tone as he leaned in. "I'm the one who can tear down your masquerade and I'm the one who drives you wild. You're ashamed that you respond to me."

She swallowed hard as she fought the urge to draw him closer. "That's not true," she whispered.

"It's okay, Jodie." Stergios dipped his head and his mouth brushed her ear. Her breath hitched in her throat as she inhaled his scent, his heat. She was surrounded by him. "That's how I feel when I'm with you. And I still can't stop myself. I don't want to."

He slid his hands in her hair, his fingers gripping the back of her head. She flattened her hands against his chest, determined to push him away when he claimed her mouth with his. She gasped as the raw pleasure tore through her.

Stergios tilted her head and drove his tongue into her mouth. His rough jaw scratched her skin and her lips stung under his forceful kiss. Jodie clawed at his shirt as she drew him in deeper. She shivered when she heard Stergios's groan of pleasure.

He bunched her hair in his hands as he devoured her with a ferocious hunger. Hot excitement crawled up her chest as she went wild under his touch. Jodie clung to his shoulders, bucking her hip against him.

Stergios suddenly wrenched away from her. He looked stunned as he gulped for air. Shell-shocked. Just like the last time, Jodie thought miserably as the throbbing lust tormented her.

She didn't want him to stop and yet she didn't have the courage to reach out for him. Her legs trembled and she stared at his face that tightened with anger and primal need. Stergios Antoniou was bad for her. He didn't care about her. He felt no respect. He was ashamed of this attraction. But right now she didn't care. She knew she would later.

Stergios turned away. "Go back to your room," he said hoarsely as he walked back to the kitchen table, his movements stiff and reluctant. "And lock the door."

CHAPTER FIVE

THE NEXT MORNING Stergios stood by the windows as he gripped the satellite phone in his hand. He watched the storm with a sense of resignation as he considered his options. There were none. He had been caught in his own net. He was being punished for what he had done.

Pain throbbed in his head and his eyes felt gritty. It had been so long since he had a hangover and it had been reckless to dull his senses around Jodie. Instead of drinking himself into a stupor, he had wasted no time in kissing her.

Stergios tensed when he heard the wheels of Jodie's suitcase drag along the stone floor. He was ready to deal with her. Last night he had pulled himself from the brink of disaster. If he hadn't pulled back, he would have taken Jodie to bed.

"I'm ready to leave," she announced as she stood next to the door.

He turned and saw Jodie in high heels and an aquamarine sheath dress. She was the epitome of cool elegance. Her beauty captured his imagination and yet it was too careful. Too perfect. He yearned to see the spark in her blue eyes. It had often given him a kick of anticipation because he'd known she was about to do something daring.

"We have a problem," he said and watched her shoulders tense as if she was ready to argue. "The weather is too severe for travel."

Jodie's eyes narrowed. "I don't believe you."

Stergios clenched his jaw. He was unaccustomed to anyone questioning his word. He gestured at the window. "Look outside."

She glanced out the window. "It's not that bad. You're making this up. You will stop at nothing to keep me away from your family."

"I want nothing more than to get you out of my home, *pethi mou*." He rubbed his hands over his eyes. "I would swim to the Volakis Island if it meant getting you out of here, but we are just going to have to suffer each other's company."

She crossed her arms and looked away. "For how long?"

"Possibly until tonight." *If they were fortunate.*

"I promised I will get you to the wedding and I will."

"I've decided not to go to the wedding," she said quietly. "I want to return to Athens and then go back to New York."

"Why?" She had been insistent that she needed to attend the wedding. She had been in a panic when he had delayed her. "What has changed?"

"Nothing." Jodie walked over to the fireplace and perched on the sofa's armrest.

"I was right," he said as he followed her. "You had been out for revenge. But this detour ruined your plans."

Jodie rolled her eyes. "You are obsessed with this idea of revenge. Why do you think I want revenge on your family? Because of how I have been treated?"

There was some truth to that. He was not proud of how his family behaved. Jodie had been young and vulnerable and they made her feel unwanted. If he had been in the same position, he would have wanted some payback. "Your father didn't shield you. Instead of revenge you want to repair your relationship with him. It doesn't make sense to me."

"I was never close to my parents and I've been estranged from my father for four years. My mother wasn't able to bond with me from the beginning." Jodie looked at the floor, her cheeks turning bright red as she revealed the truth. "I thought I had come to accept that this is the way our family interacted. But then Mom died unexpectedly of a heart attack."

"And you felt the loss of what could have been," he murmured. He had those unguarded moments after his father died in prison.

She gave a sharp nod. "I'm twenty-two and I know it's too late to get the parents I needed when I was a child. But I wanted some family connection before it was too late."

"Gregory Little doesn't know how to be a father," Stergios decided.

"I know," Jodie said as she idly swung her foot. "But it would mean a lot to me if my father was interested in what was happening in my life. If he called or visited me. Included me in a family celebration." Her foot stopped as she exhaled sharply. "Anything that would make me feel like I'm not alone and forgotten."

Stergios frowned. "That's all you want?"

"You wouldn't understand." She blinked rapidly and dabbed her fingertips against the corner of her eye. "You are surrounded by family. They are involved in every part of your life, whether you want it or not. They care about you and, in return, you protect them. That's what I want."

"You want my family to take care of you? Protect you?" Had his mother been right? Did Jodie secretly want to be an Antoniou?

"No, no, no," Jodie said with a small smile. "I don't want to be part of your family. I want to be part of *mine*."

"Going to New York won't make that happen."

"It's not going to happen wherever I am. I ambushed my father and he's on guard." She tilted her head back and gave a groan of regret. "I approached the so-called reunion the wrong way and I can't repair it."

"Your plan is to walk away and act as if Gregory doesn't exist?" That didn't sound like something Jodie would do. She was the most tenacious person he knew.

"Yes, it's finally time to admit defeat." She dropped her hands and slowly stood up. She took a deep breath and set her mouth in a determined smile. "Look on the bright side, Stergios. After tonight, we will never cross paths again."

This was what he wanted. Needed. Yet Stergios fought back the bleakness as he imagined a future without Jodie. Instead of the peace he craved, his world was colorless and deathly quiet.

Stergios shook his head, ridding himself of the image. That didn't make sense. Life would return to normal once Jodie was gone. It would be better. He silently walked back to the window, knowing that the pilot couldn't get here fast enough.

Jodie's head jerked up as the lights flickered. She checked her watch for the hundredth time. Night had fallen and there was no update from the pilot.

She nervously bit her lip and stared at the flames dancing in the fireplace. The helicopter had to show up and take her away. She wasn't going to be stuck here for another night. Alone with Stergios.

As Jodie watched him through her lashes, Stergios prowled around the room, glaring at the crashing waves and torrential rains. Throughout the day the tension between them had ebbed and flowed. One moment they could talk easily and share a laugh. And then, quite suddenly, the atmosphere would change. The tension between them now stretched until she swore it shook.

Jodie rubbed her thumb against her lips. She shouldn't have let that kiss happen but she couldn't resist another taste of the passion she'd experienced long ago. She had found her response alarming and she had been on edge all day.

Stergios probably thought she responded that way with every man. But she had been celibate for a long time and no man intrigued her enough to take him to her bed. She was determined to wait for a man who cared about her. A man she could trust with her body and heart.

Stergios wasn't that man, Jodie decided as she fought with the weight of disappointment. She watched him lean his shoulder against the window. He had proven it that night four years ago.

"Where did you go after you left the wine cellar?" Jodie cringed as the words spilled from her mouth. She knew better than to bring up that night.

He stared broodingly through the window. "As far away as I could."

It suddenly occurred to her and she looked around. "You came here, didn't you?"

Stergios hesitated. "Why would you think that?"

She burrowed deeper into the couch and stared at the fire. "This is your getaway. Your sanctuary."

"Doesn't feel like it," he muttered.

"It's isolated here. Secluded. With all communication cut off, this is the only place you will find solitude. That's why you didn't know I was banished until it was too late," Jodie said with a sigh as the truth hit her. Stergios wouldn't have abandoned her like that if he had known.

"I should have stayed and protected you." His voice was heavy with regret.

Jodie wished he had stayed but she'd instinctively understood that he had been fighting demons of his own. That was why she had lied to protect him. It had been her turn to take care of him. "What did you do while you were here?"

"Went quietly insane," he said softly.

She frowned at his serious tone. "Why?"

He gave her an incredulous look. "Do I have to spell it out? I had taken advantage of a vulnerable girl. A virgin. My stepsister. What kind of man does that?"

She raised her hand to stop that train of thought. "Okay, first of all, I was an adult at the time. A woman. And I was not vulnerable."

"I took your virginity," he said in a growl. "I'm not proud of that."

His words shouldn't hurt so much. That moment had been life-changing and he wanted to forget it. Erase that night completely. "You didn't take it," she argued hotly. "I gave it to you."

He pushed away from the window. "You had no say in the matter."

"Yes, I did!" she said as she leaned forward. "You were the one I wanted. I had lusted after you."

He stopped in his tracks as his gaze sharpened.

"That's right. I lusted after you." It had been thrilling, scary and all-consuming. "It was not a crush. Not a passing interest. It was an obsession. I tried to hide it because I knew you would reject me."

"You hid it very well." He tilted his head back and closed his eyes. "It's good I didn't know."

She blinked when the lights flickered again. "Why?"

"You had become a temptation," he said as he

dragged his hands down his face. "I had done everything I could to deny myself. I left home..."

Jodie gasped. "That was why you went abroad? Because of me?"

Stergios crossed his arms as if he was holding himself back. "I knew I had to get out before I did something."

"You were only gone for a couple of months." She had been overjoyed when he had returned to Greece that summer. She hadn't questioned why he came back so soon. "What happened?"

His gaze darkened. "I came to realize that Dimos wanted you and it was only a matter of time before he made his claim. I couldn't let that happen."

"It was never going to happen because I had no interest in him." She remembered what Stergios had said about that night. *That wasn't the only reason I stopped Dimos.* Jodie's heart began to race as she made the connection. "You weren't protecting Dimos or the merger that night. You were protecting your property."

Stergios remained silent as a ruddy color stained his high cheekbones. She saw the possessive gleam in his eyes and something wicked and primal flared deep inside her.

"I did not belong to you!" she insisted. "I belong to no man!"

"*Oxi*, you belonged to hundreds."

She flinched from his cold statement. "You couldn't bear to look at me after we had sex. And what? I was supposed to wait around in case you changed your mind and wanted to bed me again?" She shook her head when she realized that was exactly what he had expected. "I moved on, Stergios, just like you did. Just because you were my first doesn't mean you own me."

Stergios clenched his jaw and she felt the anger pulse from him. The tense silence plucked at her nerves and all she could hear was the crackle of the fire. She knew she was getting into dangerous territory.

Jodie cleared her throat. "I don't think the pilot is coming for a while and I'm getting hungry." She bolted from her seat and hurried to the kitchen.

She felt Stergios was right behind her. It was as if she was being pursued. Cornered. Her skin tingled as her stomach clenched. Why wasn't he giving her space? Why didn't he stay in his separate corner now, when she needed some distance?

"You *gave* your virginity to me?" he asked hoarsely. "Why would you do that?"

She turned around suddenly and collided into his hard, muscular chest. Jodie jumped back and crossed her arms against her chest. It was a flimsy barrier against such a man.

"I shouldn't have put it that way," she said. "It makes it sound like it was a gift. Like there is some obligation or responsibility attached to it."

"There is," he said roughly.

She didn't agree with his outdated view but she knew it was useless to argue. "If that's how you felt about it, why did you give up looking for me? Why didn't you ask me to marry you?"

"Would you have accepted?" he shot back.

"It's hard to say." Jodie fought for an inscrutable expression. She would have accepted. Without question or hesitation. She wouldn't have cared that he didn't respect her or love her. Knowing that, it was a good thing he had stopped looking for her. "You didn't answer my question," she said huskily.

She watched the muscles twitch in his cheek.

"Any marriage with you would have been disaster!"

"You weren't thinking about our compatibility," she said as the hurt bled through her. "You thought you deserved a woman better than me. You weren't going to settle for me when you wanted a woman who shared your heritage and your status."

"My marriage will be a strategic alliance," Stergios said with no apology. "It will give my family and me unlimited power and influence. And when that happens, nothing and no one could ever harm us again."

"So it doesn't matter what kind of woman you marry?" She didn't believe it. Stergios would want a "good girl" for a bride. Someone sweet and obedient.

"I need a wife who doesn't cause trouble," he said harshly. "A woman who can create a peaceful—"

The lights flickered and extinguished, plunging them into complete darkness.

Jodie gave a startled jump. She automatically reached out and curled her hand against his forearm. She felt his soaring tension under her fingertips. "Stergios?"

"The generator should kick on," he said in a strained voice.

She waited a few moments but the darkness remained. The wind howled outside and she heard Stergio's labored breathing. "I don't think it will," Jodie whispered.

"It has to."

He said it as a prayer. Her fingers clenched against his arm. "Or what?"

The beat of silence stretched before Stergios responded. "You don't want to know."

CHAPTER SIX

HE WAS INSTANTLY transported to the time he had been held captive. It was dark and he was shivering. The metal cuffs chafed at his wrists. Blood trickled from his mouth as fear pulsed inside him.

Jodie's fingers flexed against his arm. "Uh… Stergios?" Her voice sounded far away. "I have a confession to make. I…um…I don't do well in the dark."

Join the club, he thought as the memory dimmed. But her admission didn't sound right. He recalled how often she frolicked around the gardens at night when she didn't think anyone was watching. She had been fearless and free.

"Is it okay if I hold on to you?" she asked as she curled her arm around his.

"If you have to." Turmoil churned inside him as he broke out into a cold sweat. He didn't want to be touched. He needed to keep his distance but he couldn't deny Jodie's request.

"It's kind of dark in this kitchen, don't you think?" Jodie carefully turned them toward the door. "Can you take me back to the main room? I would feel better sitting by the fire."

He remembered the campfire his captors had gathered around every night. It was the only thing that held back the dark wilderness. But he had always been far away from the campfire and didn't get to enjoy the heat or the light.

Stergios silently walked Jodie to the main room. He was very aware of how her body brushed against his arm. Only she wasn't leaning against him. She felt strong and confident.

"I guess my problems with the dark—with nighttime, really—happened early on." Jodie's voice was soft and soothing. "I think it started at my first boarding school. It was an eerie place and the older girls told us ghost stories."

Jodie's voice went in and out but her hold on his arm remained firm. His tension diminished when he saw the glow from the fire. There were still too many shadows and dark corners, but he was able to guide Jodie to one of the sofas.

"Thank you. Would you sit with me?" she asked

as she patted the cushion next to her. "It would make me feel safer."

He reluctantly sat with Jodie even though he knew it was a bad idea. She didn't know what he was like in the darkness. It could take some time before the lights came back on.

"I got kicked out of that school a few years later," she continued as she curled up on the sofa, her dress riding up her thighs as she tucked her legs underneath her. "They had given me several chances but I wasted them all. The next school I went to was horrible. I didn't last long. Maybe a month?"

Stergios didn't look at her. He silently watched the fire as he tried to push the memories away. It had happened years ago. Some of his recollections were blurry and some were just an intense, overwhelming feeling. But there had been some moments that were razor sharp no matter how much he tried to forget.

"The school in South Africa was nice and I made some great friends there. Now, looking back, I should have tried harder to adapt."

She fell into silence. He didn't like that. He

wasn't following every word but he clung to the gentle rhythm of her voice.

"You purposely got kicked out of every boarding school," he said gruffly. "Why?"

Jodie shifted uncomfortably in her seat as if she was embarrassed. "The letters and phone calls from home had stopped," she told him. "I didn't see either of my parents during the school breaks. I was being left behind and I couldn't let that happen."

The woman was so afraid of becoming invisible. He didn't understand it. She grabbed attention wherever she went. She hadn't been in Athens for years and yet her name was still on everyone's tongue. "So you did everything you could to get your parents' attention."

"I broke every rule I could think of. I cheated on tests even when I knew the answers. I snuck boys in my room just to get caught and I planted liquor bottles where they could be found. I did whatever would require a call to my parents. Or better yet, be sent home."

"It didn't work," he murmured. Her stays at the Antoniou estate were brief and rare.

"No, it didn't. My actions had the opposite effect." There was a hint of regret in her voice. "The more stunts I pulled, the less my parents wanted anything to do with me. They sent me to places so far away that I couldn't visit home. It was as if they didn't know what to do with me. I felt abandoned."

Rejected, Stergios thought. So she pulled stunts that would create more attention.

Jodie was lost in her thoughts as she stared at the fire. "I often wondered what would have happened if I had run away from one of those schools. Would my parents have looked for me?"

"Of course they would." His response was automatic.

"You would assume that, Stergios," she said with a soft chuckle as she patted his shoulder. "But your family was different than mine. They always wanted to keep you close," she said with a longing sigh. "You knew all your relatives would do everything in their power to find you."

"True. I taunted my captors with the knowledge all the time. That the wrath of the Antoniou family was going to rain down on them." A vengeful smile tugged at the corner of his mouth. "And it did."

"And now you protect them with the same drive." Her eyes shone with admiration. "You take care of every relative no matter how faint the blood connection."

"Not Pagonis. He may have been my biological father but he had me kidnapped. All to get my mother's fortune." Stergios felt the bile rise as he thought of the man. Pagonis hadn't considered how it would traumatize his son. "He deserved to die in prison."

She rested her head against the back of the sofa and watched the flames dance in the fireplace. "I suspect you never told anyone what happened during your ordeal. You needed to spare them the details."

He gave her a startled look. Jodie understood him too well. His silence had been his way of protecting his family from the unpalatable truth. "The less they know, the better."

She stroked his clenched hand. "What happened that made you hate the dark?"

"I know the dangers that the night holds." He had overcome every one of them. "But it's nothing to what the darkness had revealed inside me."

"I don't understand."

The truth pressed against him, ready to break free, but he had learned to keep it to himself. "Everything I knew and believed in changed in one night." He spoke slowly as the words did not come easily. "We often camped in the wilderness. I had been left outdoors, chained and caged."

He remembered the metal rattle of his prison. His kidnappers liked to drag their weapons against the bars. The overwhelming clatter reverberated in his ears and he was stuck in that time and place until Jodie squeezed his hand.

"One of my captors..." Stergios paused as he tried to purge the face from his memory. "He thought I was easy prey. I was young and trapped. But I fought back."

"You had no choice," Jodie said.

The memories started to collide. It had happened quickly and he had no time to think or strategize. It had all been instinctual. "I almost killed him. I probably would have if his coconspirators hadn't stepped in."

"It was self-defense." Jodie didn't look horrified or shocked. She didn't draw back in fear. Instead she leaned closer. "You were just a child and he wanted to hurt you."

"I saw how much damage I could cause at a young age." Stergios could still feel the warm blood and hear the echoing screams. "I didn't know there was so much violence and rage inside me. That night I discovered what I could do when I am cornered."

"Why do you let people think you're afraid of the dark? It's not true."

"There's some truth in it. I avoid being in a position where I can't see potential threats. But it's easier for them to accept that I hate the dark. They don't want to dig deeper and I don't want them to know that the darkness is a trigger. It reminds me what I had to do to survive."

Their gaze connected and she didn't look away. He was caught in the depths of her blue eyes. He didn't move, didn't speak. For one infinitesimal moment, he found the peace he had been searching for.

"What happened after you fought back and wounded that man?" Jodie asked. "Your captors must have punished you."

"*Ne*, it's how I got this scar." He gestured at his mouth.

Jodie moved closer and brushed her thumb

against his lip. "It didn't stop you from fighting back again, did it?" she whispered.

Her touch broke the spell. "Careful, *pethi mou*." He wrapped his fingers around her wrist but he didn't pull her hand away. "I am no gentleman. I am an animal. I am red in tooth and claw."

There was no fear in her eyes. Jodie didn't listen to his warning. Didn't care. The tenderness in her gaze left him unsettled. He slowly set her hand away from him.

"Don't worry, Stergios. Your secret is safe with me," she promised.

He leaned forward and rested his arms on his knees. "I shouldn't have said anything."

"Why not?" she asked as she drew back. "You had to tell someone. It's not something you want to share with your family. They already feel so guilty they couldn't protect you during that time."

"I don't know why I told you." He knew it was a moment of weakness that he was going to regret.

"Because you don't see me as family," Jodie said as she rose from the sofa. "You don't need to protect me."

He gave a humorless laugh. "*Ne*, I do. You're not smart enough to be cautious around me. At times you bait me, wanting a reaction. Now you know better."

"I can take care of myself," she said as she walked to the kitchen. "And you."

Stergios scowled. That was the last thing he wanted. He did not want to rely on Jodie Little. She was unpredictable and seductive. Trouble. He was safer on his own.

Stergios woke up abruptly. He jackknifed up and looked around. He was on a sofa in the main room. There were ashes in the fireplace and light was blazing from the lamps. He glanced outside and saw that it was night. He heard the downpour outside but he didn't hear the whistle of the trees in the storm.

Checking his wristwatch, he saw it was past midnight. Stergios sat forward and rubbed his hands over his face. He didn't feel refreshed from his nap. He was mentally exhausted and on edge.

The lights must have woken him. He remembered Jodie went to bed a few hours ago after she gave up on talking with him. He had been defensive and uncommunicative. He had shared something personal, something he wouldn't have shared with anyone, and now he was waiting for the backlash.

He rose stiffly from the sofa and stretched. The way his shirt was creased, he guessed his sleep had been troubled. It usually was if he thought too much about his time in captivity.

Stergios needed to move around. Think about something else and the memories would vanish for a while. Grabbing the dirty dinner plates from the side table, Stergios walked into the kitchen. He went still when he saw Jodie by the sink.

The ivory slip she wore was innocent and seductive. It looked delicate, as if it would fall apart under his touch. Stergios swallowed hard as he noticed how the silk clung to her curves and angles. Lust smashed into him as his gaze followed the lace edge that emphasized her cleavage.

"Oh, you're awake," she said as she drank water from a glass.

His hands gripped the plates so tightly that he thought they would crack. "What the hell are you wearing?" His voice lashed in the electric atmosphere.

She glanced down. "What's wrong with it?"

He strode to the sink and tossed in the dishes.

From the corner of his eyes, he saw Jodie flinch from the loud clang. "You were going to wear that at Dimos's wedding?"

"Well, not at the ceremony." Jodie set her glass in the sink. "When I was in my room and sleeping. Alone."

He didn't believe it. That was the kind of lingerie a woman wore when she had seduction in mind. "A woman does not wear that when she's sleeping alone."

"That's enough, Stergios." She gave a tired sigh and held her hands up to stop him. "You no longer think I had my eyes on Dimos, so what gives? Are you trying to start an argument?"

He was and he hated that Jodie had called him on it. He felt exposed. To Jodie, who knew his secrets and his dreams. She knew how to hurt him and worse, how to make him feel stronger. She had the ability to be his most dangerous enemy, and the one person who stood her ground when others would retreat. He had to create some distance.

Stergios towered over her. "You think you know me, but you don't."

Instead of backing down, Jodie rose on her tiptoes and met his gaze. "From what I understand, you have a problem with what I sleep in."

"I do." His gaze flicked along the low-cut nightie. His skin burned as he imagined trailing his fingers down the valley between her breasts. "What man bought it for you?"

She settled back on her feet, obviously surprised by his question. "I bought it because I like it."

"You were thinking about a man when you bought it." Jealousy, hot and corrosive, bled through him. No other man should have the privilege to see her like this.

She gave a huff of exasperation and gestured at the ivory silk. "What is it about this nightie that you find so offensive?"

"That you're in it," he bit out.

He saw the angry spark in her eyes. She set her hands on her hips and the silk pulled at her curves. His tongue cleaved to the roof of his mouth as he stared at the outline of her hard nipples. He was tempted to snap the thin straps with his fingers and watch the silk glide off her body and pool at her feet.

"Would you like me to take it off?" she asked sweetly. "Right here, right now?"

His stomach clenched as he imagined her striptease. "It's that attitude that got you banished from the Antoniou family."

Her chin jerked up. "Is that right?"

"Gregory has always been embarrassed by your sexual behavior," he told her as the lust pounded through his veins. "How many schools kicked you out because of boys? Do you think your father was proud of that?"

Her eyelashes fluttered. She wasn't prepared for these accusations and line of questioning. "But only you know that I didn't do anything with them."

"And your father wasn't surprised when you were accused of trying to seduce two men in the wine cellar," he pointed out. The anger and desire clashed inside him. "He didn't stand up for you. He knew what you were."

Her cheeks went pink. "Why is it a problem for me to have sex?" she asked.

"Have as much sex as you want." He remembered how he had claimed her in the wine cellar. Stergios's arousal was painfully swift. The sex had been unforgettable and he was never able to recapture that feeling. "In marriage. With your husband, not a revolving door of lovers."

She glared at him. "Your double standards exhaust me. Is it wrong that I liked having sex with you?"

"*Ne!* Yes!" he said through clenched teeth. His nostrils flared as he remembered how Jodie's orgasm had gone on and on. She had held nothing back.

She was telling him this because she wanted him to remember. She knew he was on edge and his good behavior could easily snap. He shouldn't have told Jodie anything about himself. She was using the information to her advantage.

"Despite what your family thinks, I am not a whore," she said as she walked past him. "I am a healthy woman with a healthy appetite for sex. Deal with it."

He watched her strut away and fought the urge to follow. To hunt. Stergios's muscles locked as he fought to remain where he stood. He was not an animal. He was not—

Stergios chased Jodie before he even realized it, his footsteps quiet as raw need ate away at him.

When he grabbed her arm, he knew he was already past the point of no return. Whirling Jodie around, Stergios slammed his mouth against hers.

CHAPTER SEVEN

HIS KISS WAS hard and punishing. Jodie tried to resist as he forced her lips open with his tongue. Stergios's hand spanned against her breast as he invaded her mouth. His possessive touch nearly undid her. Her nipple tightened as she imagined his rough hand and his inquisitive tongue roaming against her bare skin.

"No," she whispered.

"Ne," he said in a hiss before he nipped her bottom lip with the edge of his teeth.

She gasped as the bite sent stinging hot sensations throughout her body. Jodie jerked her head to the side. Her rejection didn't stop him from dragging the tip of his tongue along the curve of her throat.

Jodie pushed against his shoulders. "No, Stergios. This isn't going to happen." Her strong words were undermined by her breathless tone.

Stergios's large fingers slid against her hips.

She sensed he wanted to crush her silk slip in his hands. Desire pooled between her legs as he grabbed her bottom with a rough urgency that excited her. She couldn't stop the whimper from escaping her tight throat.

He chuckled as his lips pressed against her collarbone. Her fluttering pulse beat against his mouth. "You want it as much as I do," he said triumphantly.

She squeezed her eyes shut but she couldn't ignore the truth. She *did* want this. She wanted him more than anything else. Jodie knew she should be ashamed. She desired a man who couldn't stand the sight of her.

Stergios thrust his knee between her trembling legs and she bucked against his hard, muscular thigh. Jodie held back a sob of pleasure. She was weak against him. She didn't care what Stergios thought. She needed him deep inside her.

"You don't want this," she said in one last-ditch effort to stop this madness. "You just want to display your dominance over me." She shivered with anticipation as she imagined how he would take her. It wouldn't be making love. It would be a primal mating. "I won't let you."

"You will, *pethi mou*," he predicted as he rocked her hips harder against his thigh. "You will beg me."

No, she wouldn't. She couldn't! It was humiliating that she was hot and ready for him in an instant. She needed to salvage some of her pride. "You're doing this because you revealed too much to me," she shot back. "You don't want anyone to know you, least of all me!"

Stergios gripped the back of her head. "Open your mouth for me," he said in a rasp before he lowered his head.

She pressed her lips together but Stergios would not be denied. His kiss ignited the ferocity inside her. He knew just how to touch and excite her. Stergios had set the standard for her and no other man had made her feel like this.

Jodie wanted to go wild in his arms. She wanted all he had to offer but she was afraid. This man had almost destroyed her after the last time they were together.

"We can't do this," she said against his mouth. "We shouldn't!"

"I know." His hands clenched her waist and he suddenly lifted her up. Jodie clung to his shoulders as he wrapped her bare legs around his lean waist. She saw the raw passion in his dark eyes as he carried her to his room.

The overhead lights blazed in the master bedroom. She only caught a glimpse of the stark and modern decor before he tossed her onto his bed. The mattress was wide and low to the ground. She barely noticed the cool white sheets against her back before he tumbled on top of her. He reached for her hands, lacing his fingers with hers, and stretched her arms above her head.

She twisted underneath him. "You're going to regret this," she warned.

"You are to blame," he decided as he burrowed his face against her neck.

She stiffened. "Me?"

He let go of her hands and palmed her breasts. His touch was urgent and demanding. "You can't tolerate the idea of being invisible," he muttered as if he were in a trance.

She arched her spine as his hands rubbed her sensitive nipples. "Shut up." She shouldn't have made that confession to him.

"You used to wear the most provocative clothes at home." His voice thickened and his words began to slur as he slid his hands against her rib cage. "The boldest colors. Anything that would capture my attention. My imagination."

Her face burned hot. It was true. Had she been that obvious years ago? And she had fallen in the same pattern tonight without recognizing it. Jodie shouldn't have taunted him but she wanted him to notice her. Claim her. She had always needed to be the center of his attention. To be the most important person in his life.

But she couldn't be. She was everything he didn't want in a woman. In a wife.

"You had me in agony for years," he confessed as he shoved the hem of her slip above her hips. "When you walked into a room, I had to leave."

Her hands clenched the pillow beneath her head. What was he saying? She couldn't concentrate when he stared at her with such intensity.

He bunched the silk in his hands and revealed her abdomen. He bent down and pressed his mouth against her clenching stomach. His warm breath wafted over her skin and she shivered. "If we were at the dinner table, I had to sit where I couldn't see you."

Her chest rose and fell as he tore the slip off

her body. She was splayed out before him. His for the taking. She writhed under his touch, the anticipation overwhelming.

"I found no reprieve," he continued as he took her breast into his mouth.

Jodie tossed her head from side to side as he teased her unmercifully with his tongue. Just when she didn't think she could take it anymore, Stergios bit down on her tight nipple. She cried out as the fiery sensations scorched through her veins.

"You were everywhere," he whispered before he laved his tongue against her tender flesh. "In my home, in my dreams."

He reached for her other breast and pinched her nipple. Jodie arched her spine, her feet digging into the mattress, as he took her to the edge of pleasure and pain.

"But I couldn't have you. I wouldn't allow it. I knew I wouldn't be gentle or careful if I touched you." He paused. "I was right."

"I don't want you to be gentle," she insisted in a gasp. She wanted him to be reckless. She didn't want Stergios to hide any part of himself.

Savage need stretched his golden skin against

his sharp cheekbones. “Good,” he said in a growl. “Because I can’t. Not with you.”

Stergios rose from the bed and yanked off his shirt. She sat up and reached for him. She wasn’t going to be gentle, either. Jodie pressed her mouth against his V-cut abs and licked his heated skin. She smiled, the sense of power hurtling through her, as his muscles bunched under her touch.

She grasped the zipper of his jeans and dragged the rest of his clothes down his powerful thighs. He looked like a pagan god, his jaw clenched, eyes glittering with lust, as he speared his hands in her hair.

Staring at the glorious male body in front of her, she reverently encircled her fingers against his throbbing erection. He was hot and powerful under her touch. Jodie licked the tip and hummed with appreciation before she covered him with her lips.

She tasted him with a building hunger and he encouraged her in a husky, strained voice. Jodie heard him mumble something about her red lips as she pleasured him. When she drew him deep inside her mouth, Stergios’s ragged breath echoed in the bedroom. She gripped him hard when he swelled against her tongue.

Stergios grasped her jaw and stopped her before carefully pulling away. Panic filled her chest. Why was he stopping? Why did he have to come to his senses when she was aching for him? "Wait," she pleaded.

"I can't," he said in a low, driven tone. Stergios grabbed for her and turned her over. Jodie blinked, startled. She was on her hands and knees facing away from him. He slid his finger along the wet folds of her sex. Pleasure rippled through her.

He grabbed her hips, his fingers digging into her skin, and mounted her. Jodie closed her eyes as the low, guttural moan ripped from her throat. She clawed the sheets, heat blooming her skin, as he gave a deep thrust.

Jodie rolled her hips as he stretched and filled her. Stergios withdrew only to thrust harder. She urged him on and he exceeded her most brazen demands. She met his demonic pace as the bed shook beneath them.

Stergios slid his hand beneath her and found her slick clitoris. Jodie surrendered to his touch.

Her mind shut down as her climax hit. Her cries of ecstasy echoed in the room as wave after wave of white-hot pleasure swept through her.

Her flesh gripped Stergios and his thrusts grew unpredictable. Unbridled. He banded his arms around her and held her close as he surged deep inside. His chest, slick with sweat, pressed against her spine as he burrowed his face into the crook of her neck.

"Jodie!" he said in a roar as he found his release.

Her knees buckled from the force and she collapsed onto the mattress. Her arms and legs shook as she fell onto her pillow. Jodie's heart felt as if it was going to burst through her skin as she took in big swallows of air.

Every muscle pulsed and twitched. Stergios rolled to his side and silently gathered her in his arms. Jodie weakly closed her eyes as he held her close. She needed his touch but she didn't want to him to see how much the simple gesture affected her.

As she rested her head against his chest, listening to Stergios's thudding heartbeat, she tried to tell herself that this didn't mean anything. It was a moment of madness, never to be repeated.

But she couldn't lie to herself. Tonight meant *everything* to her.

Jodie stood by the bay of windows and looked out onto the beach. It was a cloudy and gray morning. There should be nothing that stood in the way of her getting off this island.

She saw her reflection in the window. Her hot-pink dress was prim with its rounded collar and short sleeves. Her black handbag hung from her forearm as she clasped her hands in front of her. The proper image was a far cry from the carnal woman last night.

Jodie felt her skin go hot as the memories overwhelmed her. She had reached for Stergios during the night and demonstrated exactly how she felt. There had been no limits to her desire. It was as if she had been parched for years and had finally found water to slake her thirst.

But when she had woken in the morning, she had been alone in her bedroom. Tucked into her bed and her torn slip carefully folded on the chair next to her. At some time around dawn Stergios had carried her into her room, as if sharing a bed for the whole night had been too intimate for him.

After she had showered and dressed, she had searched the small house and discovered Stergios was gone. His absence had been like a fist in the stomach. It was just like the last time. He had recognized how far he had fallen and couldn't get away fast enough. Only this time he wasn't able to go very far.

Jodie flinched when she heard his footsteps outside but schooled her features into a cool expression when the front door swung open. She exhaled slowly, bracing herself before she turned around to greet him.

Her heart skipped a beat when she saw him dressed in a casual white tunic and a faded pair of jeans. His hair was tangled and windswept and the stubble on his angular jaw seemed darker. She longed to walk up to him and curl against his chest. Her thought vanished when her gaze clashed with his wintry eyes. The generous lover who had kissed her breathless last night had been replaced with the cold and ruthless man.

"The helicopter will be here in ten minutes," he informed her as he set down the satellite phone.

"The pilot has been instructed to take you to Athens."

"Thank you." She gestured at the suitcase by the door. "I'm packed and ready."

The silence stretched between them. Stergios started to pace the room but kept his distance from her. He couldn't have made it more obvious that he wished she were already gone.

As she watched him prowl the room, Jodie knew she should feel some sense of feminine pride. She could make the great Stergios Antoniou fall to his knees. But she didn't feel victorious. Stergios didn't like her. He wished he didn't want her. He couldn't stand being next to her.

"Are you okay?" she blurted out. "Last night after the power outage..." He cast a scathing look and she stumbled into silence. It was a mistake to mention his moment of vulnerability.

"I'm fine," he said tersely. "And you?"

She gave an abrupt nod. She didn't trust herself to speak.

"You can't be," he decided, his voice a rasp. "I can see the whisker burns on your skin from here.

There were faint scratches all over her body.

He had marked her in more ways than one. “And I see a love bite on your neck.”

He raked his hands through his long hair. “That’s different.”

No, it wasn’t. Jodie turned her attention back to the beach before she started an argument. He had encouraged her to explore his body in the middle of the night. Nothing she did or said had shocked him. But did he find her desire for him unseemly in the light of day? Should her lust not match his?

She guessed she was supposed to be innocent, passive and fragile. Right now she felt fragile. She felt as if she was going to burst into tears.

Stergios took a few ground-eating strides to reach her. “Give me your cell phone,” he said as he stretched out his hand.

She automatically took a step back. “I don’t think so,” she said as she held her purse close to her body.

His eyebrows rose in surprise and her fingers tightened on the leather. Did Stergios expect unquestioning obedience after she had yielded completely to him last night? “I want to add my number to your contact list.”

Jodie stared at him. “Why?”

His lips compressed into a line. “I will need to know if there were any consequences from last night.”

“There won’t be.”

“How can you be so sure? Are you on the pill?”

“Well, no…” There had been no reason for her to have a prescription.

His shoulders hunched as the harsh lines of his face deepened. It looked as if he had the world on his shoulders. Had he felt this way four years ago when they first had made love?

She raised her hands as if she could soothe his troubled thoughts. “You have nothing to worry about.”

“You’re wrong.” There was a bite of anger in his voice. “If you get pregnant, everything I have worked for all these years will disappear.”

Jodie went still. It hurt that she was a distraction, a hindrance to his dreams, but how would her presence in his life ruin everything? “What are you talking about?”

“Do you know the fight I would have on my hands if I had a baby out of wedlock? A love child with my stepsister?” His face was ashen.

"The board of directors would crucify me. The scandal would damage the Antoniou Group. I would be forced to marry you and I can't let that happen. When I marry, it will be to strengthen my family's power base, not because of a mistake."

Jodie bent her head and stared at the ground. He sought for extraordinary power so no one could harm him and he would use marriage to get it. Jodie wanted him to feel safe even if it meant he had to stay away from her. Peace was the one thing she couldn't give him. She never could.

There was one thing she could do for him. She could leave and never come back. Sever all connections. Jodie winced as she imagined the hole it would leave in her heart. But she had to let go of Stergios so he could find what he needed.

What they both needed, she amended. Because he would marry for power and she would marry for love. Whatever this was that they shared wouldn't last. She wouldn't waste his time or hers anymore.

"I expect you to call me whether or not you're pregnant." His hands were bunched at his sides.

"If you don't I will hunt you down and get my answer."

It would be a repeat of what happened last time. Only this time she would know that he was pursuing her. And she'd let him catch her. And if he found her again, they would fall back into bed and the cycle would continue. Jodie twisted her lips. He would be drawn to her and hate the power she had over him. It wouldn't stop him unless he thought she had fallen into bed with another man.

Another man. Jodie lifted her head. What if she said another man had a claim on her? Her pulse started to race. *No, no, no.* She couldn't do it. It would be too painful. The ultimate betrayal in Stergios's eyes. She immediately discarded the idea. If she told that lie, Stergios would cut her out of his life for good.

Which was what she wanted, didn't she? She had to end this relationship before it became an unhealthy obsession that changed the course of their lives. But if she did this, there was no turning back. Stergios would never forgive her.

Which was why she had to go through with it. It was the only way. Her mouth was dry and she nervously licked her lips. "Like I said, you don't have anything to worry about," she said in a whisper. She wasn't sure if she could do this.

He gave an impatient sigh. "How would you know?"

Her heart pumped hard and her stomach twisted. The room tilted and she fought back the nausea. She could do this. All she had to do was lie and make a clean getaway. Just a few words and she could end this madness.

"Jodie?"

She struggled to meet his curious gaze. "Because I'm already pregnant." She forced out the next words as she spread her hands against her stomach. "With another man's child."

CHAPTER EIGHT

"THEN...*KATALAVÉNO*? I don't understand." His mind lagged behind but the pain had been sharp and swift. There was another man in Jodie's life. And she...Stergios refused to believe it. "What did you say?"

"I'm—" her voice hitched "—already pregnant."

Pregnant. She was with child. *Another man's child.* The bitterness cut through him like acid. He studied her slim figure in the hot-pink dress. *"Oxi,"* he said in a whisper. "I don't believe you."

She lifted her chin. "Why would I lie about something like this?"

Stergios couldn't move. He felt as if he'd been hacked down from where he stood. Pregnant. She couldn't be pregnant. No, Jodie was *his*.

A chill settled into his bones. Stergios remembered feeling like this before. The numbness held back the searing pain so he could cope. Survive.

The coldness would be temporary and then the ferocious rage would take over. "Who's the father?"

She appeared surprised by the question. "That is none of your business."

"Do you know?" His voice was flat.

She jerked back as if she'd been slapped. "I'm going to ignore that."

"Do. You. Know?" He bared his teeth as he enunciated the words.

She pressed her lips together and crossed her arms.

"You don't know," he said in a stunned breath. How could she do this? Stergios thought he knew Jodie. "Was he a stranger? Or were there a few other candidates at that time?"

She glared at him before she turned away. "I'm so glad I shared this news with you."

Other pieces of the puzzle started to fall into place. The anger and despair swirled and clashed inside him. "This is why you no longer drink," he said in a low voice as he struggled to control his emotions. "And why you suddenly have this interest in family."

She gave a start as if she couldn't believe he

had put the pieces together. "It isn't sudden," she said over her shoulder.

Stergios bunched his hands in his hair as his heart thudded against his ribs. "I couldn't understand why you wanted to reconcile with your father," he said as he searched his memory for other signs. "I thought it was for revenge. I couldn't figure it out. I didn't think..."

She refused to look at him. She should be ashamed, he decided. This woman was his. He knew Jodie made no promises to him but this felt like a betrayal. Stergios didn't think she could have hurt him like this. He couldn't forgive her actions.

He dragged his hands down to his sides. "You bitch."

Her spine stiffened but she didn't turn around. "I'm going to wait at the helipad," she announced as she marched to the door.

Stergios watched her. How could she be hard and emotionless now when she had been open and loving last night? "What did your father say?"

Jodie slid to a stop and whirled around. "He

doesn't know. No one knows." She pointed at Stergios. "Do not say a word to him."

"Why not?" Why would she hide something like this from Gregory? Would her father disapprove of the man?

"Because..." Jodie spluttered as pink tinged her cheeks. The unfeeling woman was suddenly flustered. "Because it's...customary to wait until the first trimester before you make the announcement."

Something wasn't right. He didn't know if he should trust his instincts but he didn't believe her explanation. "How far along are you?"

She grabbed her suitcase and concentrated on raising the handle. "Not far."

"But you knew you were pregnant. You knew and you spread your legs for me," he said with disgust. "You let me..."

"Stop it, Stergios."

He wasn't going to listen to Jodie's pleas. She had lost that right. The destructive anger flashed inside him before he tamped it down. "If you weren't pregnant, I would..."

"Would what?" she asked, tilting her head as

she watched the tremors sweep his body. "No need to hold back, Stergios. What would you do?"

He wasn't sure how he'd respond and that scared him. He would hunt down the mysterious father and destroy him. He would pray that the baby wouldn't inherit Jodie's treachery and manipulation. And Jodie? He would cast her out of his life for good.

Starting now. Stergios ruthlessly controlled the pain threatening to erupt, knowing he had to be emotionless if he was going to retaliate. "I'm grateful that you're pregnant."

Jodie took one step back and watched him as if he was a predatory animal who was ready to go in for the kill. "What do you mean?"

"Because that means you will never have my baby," he explained in a disquieting tone. "I'm grateful that my child wouldn't have you for a mother. A whore, a liar and an outcast."

She paled. "Yes, it's a very good thing that you are not the father."

She wasn't fighting back. Stergios wanted her to. He didn't want to see her eyes glistening with unshed tears. He needed answers. "The mother of my child would be—"

"Pure?" she offered. "Compliant?"

"My children deserve a good mother," he said as his gaze raked over her. "A woman they could respect and trust. A woman who could make them proud."

Her eyes darkened but she kept her mouth firmly shut. "Goodbye, Stergios," she finally said and she reached for the door.

"Who's the father?" he said in a roar.

Her shoulders slumped for a moment. And then, as if she had made a decision, she grabbed the doorknob as if it was a lifeline. "The only thing you need to know is that it's not you."

He was suddenly behind her and flattened his hand against the door so she couldn't open it. He wanted her gone and yet he wanted to dole out her punishment. His world was crashing down around him and the woman who destroyed it was walking away without a backward glance.

Jodie kept her head bent. "I hear the helicopter. Please let me leave."

"What do you plan to do? Are you keeping the baby?"

She glanced up at him, horrified. "What are you recommending I do?" Her voice was unsettling and he lowered his hand. "Why wouldn't I keep the baby? Because it's an inconvenience for you? Because it isn't *yours*?"

Did she think he was that kind of monster? His stomach twisted with dread. Jodie had seen him at his worst and this is what she thought of him?

"The sight of you sickens me. Get out," he said in a threatening growl. "Get out of my house and out of my sight. Get the hell out of my life."

"I will, Stergios. As fast as I can."

Jodie leaned back in her chair and looked outside the window of her apartment. She had always enjoyed New York City in the autumn but lately she had struggled to see the beauty. There was a crisp bite to the late October weather and the leaves were turning crimson and gold, but all she wanted to do was hibernate.

"The apartment is just as I remembered."

She turned her attention to her father. He sat across from her at the small table as if he had all the time in the world. *This wasn't happening*, she thought in a daze but his fading blond hair gleamed under the chandelier. She watched numbly as he reached for a scone from the tiered cake stand.

Why was he here? What did he want? She thought cynically. She hadn't been able to hide her astonishment when he had called her in the morning and wanted to drop by.

"You haven't changed a thing from when your mother lived here," he remarked.

"No, I'm not ready to handle that big of a project," Jodie murmured. She had inherited the penthouse apartment months ago but she didn't feel settled. This wasn't home. Growing up, she had always used it as a layover.

"You look pale," Gregory Little said as he took a sip of his tea. "Have you been ill?"

No, she was heartbroken but she didn't dare tell that her father. The man liked to gossip and she didn't want it getting back to Stergios. No one needed to know that she had difficulty eating and sleeping. She couldn't focus. Some days it felt as if time went too fast and other days it dragged on.

It was painful loving someone who didn't love her back. The burden weighed heavily on her like a cloak. She had felt unloved and unwanted many times in her life. She thought she was used to it, but Stergios's disgust and hatred had knocked her back.

"I've been tired since returning from Greece," she admitted as she reached for her teacup. "There were some people sick on the plane. I'm probably fighting off something like a cold."

"That's why you should have your own plane."

She gave a wry smile at his response. Gregory Little had become accustomed to the Antoniou way of life. He would do anything to protect his standard of living.

"Or were you concerned after the helicopter's mechanical problem?" he asked. "That was a rare occurrence. I can't recall it happening before."

Mechanical problem? Jodie frowned until she remembered the lie about why she had missed the wedding. "It does make me hesitate," she said smoothly. "So, have Dimos and Zoi returned from their honeymoon?"

"Yes, Dimos is now vice president but it will be a long adjustment period for him," he predicted. "He doesn't have the stamina to carry the same workload as Stergios."

Jodie flinched when she heard Stergios's name.

She clearly remembered the raw fury in his eyes when she had left. That man hated her. She kept trying to tell herself that it was for the best.

"And…Stergios?" She tried to sound casual but she craved for any news or information about him. "How is he?"

Gregory frowned as he took a sip of his tea. "Mairi is worried about him. He has always been a workaholic but it's gotten much worse. But, then, he is finalizing the Antoniou-Volakis merger. I'm sure he will take some time off once that is done."

Stergios had dived right into his work after she'd left. The knowledge wounded her. It was as if their weekend had been a blip in his calendar. He had gone on with his life as if nothing had happened.

"I probably shouldn't tell you since it hasn't been announced," Gregory said as he lowered his voice, "but he's going to get engaged."

Jodie felt her skin go cold as her stomach heaved. Her cup clattered against her saucer. *Engaged.* The word echoed in her mind. Stergios was getting engaged.

"Sorry," she said weakly as she carefully let

go of her cup before she broke the delicate handle between her fingers. "That just caught me by surprise. Stergios doesn't strike me as someone who is ready to settle down."

He had met someone special... He belonged to another... He was going to make this woman his wife... A bitter taste filled her mouth and she swallowed roughly.

"He's been playing with the idea of an Antoniou-Diamantopoulos merger for the past year," Gregory Little continued, oblivious to her unnatural stillness.

"Diamantopoulos?" she interrupted.

"Aleka Diamantopoulos," Gregory added. "The shipping heiress."

That didn't narrow it down much for Jodie. She frantically searched her memory until she remembered the quiet woman who played the piano with precision but no passion. Jealousy coiled around her heart and squeezed so hard that she wanted to double over.

"I think I remember her," she murmured. Aleka was sweet and obedient. Young and virginal. Just Stergios's type, she decided uncharitably. "Lovely girl."

"And the alliance between families will make the Antonious very powerful."

"That's…wonderful." Jodie smiled wanly. She folded her hands on her lap as the sense of loss swept through her. Perhaps all of those finishing schools had finally served their purpose. No one would be able to tell that she felt breakable. As if she was going to splinter into a million pieces and she would never be whole again.

Stergios was getting everything he wanted. She should be pleased with the turn of events. He was gaining the power and the security to protect his family. Soon he would find the peace he craved. It was everything she couldn't give him.

She stared at her manicured hands as her mind spun. She had done the right thing when she cut off all connection with Stergios. She had regretted lying to him about being pregnant. So many times she had been tempted to call him and tell him the truth.

But the cycle, the obsession, would have continued. She would have wasted a lifetime wanting to be with a man who didn't think she was worthy of him.

"Jodie?" Her father's voice pierced through her troubled thoughts. "What do you think?"

She jerked her head up and saw Gregory's look of expectation. "I'm sorry?"

Annoyance flickered in her father's blue eyes. "I'm inviting you to come to Greece for Christmas."

Jodie froze as the words replayed in her head. "Why?" she blurted. She gasped with horror and tried again. "I mean—"

He gave an understanding nod. "I shouldn't have allowed this much time to pass between us. I want to make a fresh start. What better time than Christmas?"

"But when I showed up in Athens earlier..." Her voice trailed off. What had changed? Why did he come to this conclusion now when he didn't make any overtures when she last saw him?

"I avoided you." Gregory bent his head and nervously crumbled the scone between his fingers. "You suddenly appeared and we thought you were planning to cause trouble. We should have recognized that you were still grieving the loss of your mother and needed to be around family."

"We?" she asked dully. She should have known her stepmother had a say in this.

"You know, Mairi and me," he explained. "And Stergios."

"Stergios?" She stiffened her spine. She couldn't imagine how he had poisoned her father's opinion of her. "What does he have to do about this?"

"He recommended I drop by and check on you once I finished my trip in Toronto." Gregory Little shrugged. "He acted as if it was urgent but you seem fine."

She didn't understand. How would that punish her? Jodie's head ached as she tried to understand his strategy. Did he think her father would drop by and notice her pregnant belly? Why would he care? Why did he bother? Jodie knew she was dead to him.

"Do you already have plans for Christmas?" her father asked.

"Some invitations have already trickled in but I haven't made any commitments." None of the traditional gatherings had interested her. But the promise of spending the holidays with family? It was something she had yearned for over the past few years and it was too good to pass up. "Who all will be there?"

"All of the family and a few close friends. Shall I expect you?"

Jodie bit her lip, her heart pounding against her chest, as she considered her options. She was afraid to accept. If she said yes, it meant she would have to see Stergios. But if she said no, she knew her father would not extend this kind of invitation again.

"I would love to, Dad," she said with a smile. "I can't wait."

CHAPTER NINE

JODIE CLENCHED THE banister and slowly descended the grand staircase of the Antoniou estate. Holiday decorations swathed the limestone walls and the tallest, fattest Christmas tree sat in the center of the entrance hall. She heard a harp being played in the music room and watched the other guests stand around and chat as they drank the finest champagne.

Her silver dress sparkled under the chandeliers but she wasn't in a festive mood. She pressed her lips as she searched the well-dressed crowd. Her heart stopped and she jolted with surprise when she saw Stergios.

His dark hair was shorn and ruthlessly tamed, emphasizing the sleek shape of his head. Stergios's angular jaw was clean-shaven and his dark suit fitted his sleek, athletic body. He had tamed the wildness within. He was a commanding presence, a man who ruled all he could see.

When his lips tilted in a tender smile, Jodie stared at the transformation on his face. He looked younger. Happy. It took her a moment to realize that look was for the woman next to him. Aleka Diamantopoulos. Jodie's stomach heaved; she watched as the young woman shyly blossomed under Stergios's attention.

He had never smiled like that. Not at her. She hadn't made him that happy or content. Jodie wanted to look away but she couldn't. She took in a reedy breath as her body tensed with jealousy. What was so special about Aleka?

Jodie didn't see an engagement ring on the shipping heiress's finger but she knew it was only a matter of time. She looked away as the dull, aching pain coiled her chest. A giant solitaire representing Stergios's wealth, status and power was probably gift wrapped and tucked in his jacket.

She knew she should have canceled this trip but she didn't want to. She couldn't. Not only would it make it unlikely that she'd get another invitation, but there was something she had to do in person.

She glanced in Stergios's direction again and saw him staring at her. His smile disappeared and she shrank back from his contemptuous gaze. Jodie turned abruptly and regretted it. She squeezed her eyes shut and fought for balance. She knew better than to make sharp turns. Or wear stiletto heels.

Or visit Athens, she thought. The doctor had given her permission to travel, but it was courting disaster. But she had to see Stergios one last time.

Because she was carrying his baby.

Panic fluttered in her veins and she splayed her hand against her stomach. Six weeks ago she had discovered she was pregnant. At first she'd been thrilled and shared the news with her closest friends. But she had been reluctant to inform Stergios.

How could she tell him? She had made such a mess of things. Jodie bowed her head as the tears pricked her eyes. She had lied to Stergios and made claims so he would stay away. Her decisions had turned out to be for the best. Stergios was getting the life he wanted and the wife he needed. An unexpected pregnancy would change all of that.

"Damn, Jodie," Dimos said as he walked by her and stopped. "You look like hell."

"How sweet of you to notice." Her tone was acidic but she knew he spoke the truth. It had been another reason why she had been reluctant to show up at the Antoniou home for Christmas. She didn't want to be remembered like this with her pallor, limp hair and constant tiredness. She had her pride and she wanted Stergios to eat his heart out. Now he was probably thinking he got a clean getaway.

Jodie forced her attention on Dimos and noticed he wasn't looking his best, as well. He looked older with his puffy face and bloodshot eyes. "I understand you've been working around the clock." Concern threaded in her voice. "Doesn't Stergios know you're a newlywed?"

"Let me give you a piece of advice." Dimos swilled his drink. "Consider all of your options before you get married."

Understanding dawned on her. Dimos was staying late at the office so he could avoid going home. "No need to give me advice. I will never marry."

Dimos snorted. "That's what they all say."

"No, seriously. I have no reason to do so. There is no family or financial pressure."

"Lucky you," he said bitterly as he darted a glance in the direction of his wife on the other side of the room. "What about love that you used to spout on about? You had a strong romantic streak in your teen years."

"No, that streak is long gone," she said in a whisper. She used to think she would only marry for love but she had an idealized version of it. Now she knew that love didn't bring her joy or happiness. It didn't fulfill her or give her a sense of purpose. Love brought her confusion and pain. She had the ability to love but she was incapable of being loved. Marriage or a committed relationship was not in her future.

"What guy changed your mind? You'd always talked about having a family."

"It doesn't mean I have to marry or stay with one man." It was what she wanted, but she had to be realistic. Once she had imagined having a loving husband and many children but she needed to modify her definition of family.

Dimos's eyes gleamed with interest. "That's true, monogamy is an outdated and unnatural idea."

Jodie raised her hand. "No, that—"

"Let's hope Zoi doesn't hear you," Stergios said next to Jodie.

Jodie stiffened and her skin tingled at the sound of his husky voice. She wasn't prepared to see Stergios. To be this close without touching him. She tried to remain calm but the agony of what she had lost roiled through her stomach.

Dimos's face turned a deep red. For a moment Jodie thought he was going to launch into a tirade. Instead he closed his mouth with a snap and marched away.

"Do you look for trouble or does it come naturally?" Stergios asked Jodie.

"I didn't say anything about cheating or having affairs."

Stergios looked at his cousin over his shoulder. "Then how did Dimos get that into his head?"

"I have no idea how his mind works."

"Sure you do. He always thinks about sex when you're around." His mouth twisted in displeasure as he noticed how the silver dress hugged her burgeoning curves. "And you were seeing if you still have the sexual allure over him."

"No!"

Stergios's gaze dropped to her stomach. "Have you told him that you're pregnant?"

Her heart stopped and she felt so light-headed she thought she was going to collapse onto the floor. She gave a ragged breath when she remembered that Stergios didn't know the whole truth.

"Probably not," he said with a sneer. "That would change everything. He would run in the other direction and you would have no power over him."

"Don't compare his reaction with yours." She had to tell him about the baby, but how? Where did she start? He wasn't going to believe her and she wasn't up for a battle.

Stergios crossed his arms and studied her. "Why am I the only person you've told?"

She gave an awkward shrug, not sure how to answer that. It did look strange that she had confided in him. "You should be honored."

"You haven't told Gregory and you're past the first trimester."

She gave him a sharp look. "Is that why you manipulated my father into visiting me? So he would see that I was pregnant?"

"Oxi." Surprise flickered in his dark eyes. "No,

pethi mou," he said quietly. "I had him visit you because you shouldn't be alone at this time in your life."

She blinked, dumbfounded, her lips parting as she watched Stergios walk away. Jodie clasped her hands in front of her as she felt the tears burn behind her eyes. She didn't know why she was getting emotional. She was used to being alone in the world. She just wasn't used to someone noticing her predicament. Or caring. Or reaching out. She had immediately slapped him away, thinking it was a trick.

She was tempted to follow Stergios and apologize. Her heartbeat pounded in her ears. She should tell him everything now before she lost her courage.

Jodie suddenly felt hot stinging needles prick her skin as perspiration blanketed her. She clapped her hand over her mouth, knowing she was going to be sick.

Her bedroom was too far away. Jodie briskly walked to the door that led to the portico. She stepped outside and welcomed the coldness against her skin. Leaning against the heavy stone column, she took in big gulps of the night air.

Her legs felt shaky as she took the steps down to the terrace. She needed to compose herself before she went back inside. No one was going to notice if she was absent. For once, being invisible had its benefits.

The party had drifted into the music room. Stergios searched the crowd that had already broken into the usual groups and cliques. The older generation was on one side of the room while the younger relatives were sitting together and checking their phones.

Servants in black jackets and white gloves were serving champagne and dessert on silver platters. He noticed Aleka was at the grand piano playing traditional Christmas carols. Jodie was nowhere to be found.

Stergios tapped Gregory on the shoulder. "Have you seen Jodie?"

"Hmm? Jodie?" Gregory lifted his head and looked around the room as if he was just now noticing his daughter's absence. "She's somewhere around here. Probably playing billiards," he said, preoccupied, as he motioned for one of the waiters.

"*Oxi*, she's not." He had already checked the billiards room. "I saw her step outside but she hasn't come back."

"She's fine," Gregory studied the desserts on the silver tray the waiter presented. The scent of oranges, cinnamon and cloves wafted in the air. "She's probably walking around the garden. She does that a lot."

Stergios had always thought the man was a lazy father but hadn't Gregory noticed the changes in his daughter? Didn't he care? She was pale, quiet, and the shadows under her eyes suggested she wasn't sleeping. Jodie was trying to hide the symptoms of her pregnancy and Stergios didn't know why she bothered making the attempt.

"It's been twenty minutes since she stepped outside," he said as he checked his watch.

"There's nothing to worry about," Gregory said as he chose a *melomakarona* cookie that always made Stergios think of Christmas. "We have the best security system on the grounds. If she's fallen and hurt herself, she can push one of the security buttons."

Hurt. His chest tightened with dread. Jodie could be hurt and in pain.

Stergios ran out of the room and into the entrance hall. He scanned the area and saw that Jodie still wasn't there. He stepped outside and onto the portico. The cold air slapped at his skin as the darkness enveloped him. Stergios hesitated, his breath caught in his throat, as he pushed away the memories of the pitch-black wilderness.

There were no Christmas lights on the grounds and the moon was hidden behind clouds. Taking the steps two at a time, Stergios stood on the terrace that was streaked with the weak light from the arched windows. He looked around the side garden and didn't see the glimmer of her silver dress.

"Jodie?" he called, his voice echoing in the cold air, but she didn't reply.

Stergios launched down the gravel path, the roar of his blood loud in his ears. He didn't care if there were security cameras and emergency buttons. He knew what the darkness held. He was aware of how a quiet night could turn dangerous.

He surged unseeingly down the path, driven by the memory of being hunted as a little boy and the terror that had overwhelmed him. Stergios flinched when his broad shoulders caught on a branch. He paused and took a deep breath before he continued. Relief and anger swirled inside him when he saw a faint gleam of silver.

Jodie was slumped on the ground, her arms and head resting on a stone bench. She weakly lifted her head when she heard him approach. "Stergios?" she said in a croak.

"You fool," he muttered as he pulled off his jacket in clumsy, urgent moves. His hands were rougher than he intended when he draped it around her shoulders. "What were you thinking?"

"I was sick and wanted to be alone." She gasped when he lifted her into his arms. "Why did you come looking for me?"

"What kind of question is that?" he asked tautly.

"You can't stand the sight of me," she said as she huddled into his warm suit jacket. "I've caused you nothing but trouble."

"Don't remind me." The memories of the wilderness were beginning to swarm and he needed to get back to the house before he couldn't fight them back anymore.

"You searched for me." She reached up and cupped her hand against his cheek. "In the dark?"

"I'm not afraid of the dark," he said in a withering tone as he kept his gaze forward. "I have already explained it."

"You're afraid of what the dark will trigger inside you," she said and dropped her hand before she rested her head against his shoulder. "What I will do to you."

"You don't have that power over me anymore," he said as he held her close. "You killed it the moment you slept with me when you were carrying another man's child."

Jodie gave a long sigh. "Good."

"This is an excessive use of caution, Stergios." Jodie lay back in her hospital bed and looked around the deluxe private suite. "All of the doctors agreed that I was dehydrated from traveling and that's why I got light-headed. Staying overnight for observation is unnecessary."

"You will be discharged when the doctors say it's safe."

No, when you decide it's safe, Jodie silently corrected. Everyone from the patient transporter to the Chief of Medicine had bowed down to Stergios's wishes. She suspected he was a major donor for the hospital. When he had demanded the best room for her, she had not expected this kind of medical care.

Her suite reminded her of a five-star hotel, only this stay would include a private nurse and an in-house chef. When she had been wheeled into the room with Stergios at her side, she had been surprised by the luxurious touches. The room decor was a mix of dark natural wood and a soft green color palette. The bathroom was spacious and the sitting area had sofas, chairs and a kitchenette.

She didn't need this, so why was it important that she was given the VIP treatment? Jodie watched Stergios from beneath her lashes. He was no longer acting like a chieftain on the warpath yet he was on guard for any threat or problems. The color had been restored in his high cheekbones but he still maintained a stony expression.

Stergios wanted her out of his life, so why was he acting like this? He didn't know that she was pregnant with his baby. And why did he insist that he stay with her?

"You should go home," she said gently. There was no way she would sleep if he were here. "I appreciate what you've done but you don't need to watch over me."

He gave her a curt glance. "I've already honored your request and didn't sit in during the physical exam. I am not making any more compromises."

Compromise? The man didn't understand the meaning of the word. It had been a battle getting him to leave her so she could be examined. "I'm allowed some privacy!"

"Privacy?" he repeated incredulously. "I am intimately acquainted with your body. You have nothing to hide from me." He braced his hands against the side of her bed and leaned forward. "Although you are acting suspicious."

Jodie gave him a startled look.

"What's going on?" he asked. He raked his eyes over her. "What did the doctors say? Why are you not taking care of yourself?"

Jodie bristled under his tone. "Don't talk to me like that. I am not neglecting my responsibilities. I am doing everything in my power to have a healthy pregnancy." She was using all of her time, energy and resources to give this child a promising start.

"Calm down, *pethi mou*." He stroked his knuckle against her jaw. "I am not accusing you of anything."

"Your job is done," she said firmly as she jerked her head away, "and you can go home and sleep."

"I will decide when I'm done looking after you."

She saw the determined glint in his dark eyes. "That tone might intimidate your employees, but it just makes me angrier," she informed him in a cool tone. "You are pushing your luck. I will call security and have you removed from this room if necessary."

He arched an eyebrow. "Why are you so uncomfortable having me here?"

"I'm not used to it," she admitted as she nervously plucked the fine linen. She had always wanted someone to care and to worry about her. She needed someone to wonder where she was and if she was okay. But now that she had it, even temporarily, she was afraid that she was going to do something to ruin it.

"You're overwrought and tired. It's time you get some sleep," Stergios ordered as he glanced at his watch. "I'm going to speak to the nurse before I leave."

"Again?" She wearily closed her eyes. "Don't scare her off."

"If she's easily scared, it's best if I know now and have a different nurse assigned to you," he said as he left the room.

Jodie sighed with relief and carefully rolled to her side so she didn't pull at the intravenous tubes. Stergios had been acting strangely over-protective since they'd arrived at the emergency room. Ordinarily she would have hated how he'd taken charge and made demands, but at the time she felt too weak to do it herself. She idly wondered how he'd act if he knew this was his baby.

She needed to tell him the truth but she was unwilling to face the aftermath. He was going to be furious. This child was going to create chaos in his orderly world.

What demands would he make? That she didn't have the baby? That she put it up for adoption?

If he tried to coerce her into giving up her baby, he would discover an epic fight on his hands. The best-case scenario was that Stergios would deny the baby's existence and keep it a secret from his family.

Jodie frowned when she heard Stergios's steady footsteps pounding against the corridor floor. She slowly turned onto her back and stared at the open door. It sounded as if he was getting closer.

He knows. Her stomach twisted and she suddenly felt queasy. *He knows about the baby.* She had waited too long to tell him.

Suddenly he was there, clenching the door frame with his hands. She forgot to breathe when her gaze connected with his blistering glare.

"You are not in your second trimester?" His voice was quietly sinister. "Your date of conception was in the last week of September?"

He surged forward and she wanted to launch out of bed. He got there before she could move. Jodie wished she could curl up in a ball and pretend this wasn't happening.

Stergios flattened his palms against the mattress. He invaded her space and she was trapped.

Surrounded. Jodie couldn't look away. She flinched when he spoke in a harsh whisper.

"When were you planning to tell me that the baby is mine?"

CHAPTER TEN

HE WAS GOING to be a father. Stergios stared at Jodie as the thud of his heart echoed in his head. His skin felt cold and clammy as his world slowly tilted. Stergios struggled to remain upright as he drew in a shallow breath. He was bringing an innocent child into this cruel and dangerous world.

Jodie lowered her gaze and turned her head to the side. "I was going to tell you."

He doubted it. If the nurse hadn't mentioned the due date, he may never have known. The possibility sent a chill down his spine. Jodie would have kept him from his child.

"When did you find out?" he asked in a snarl.

She swallowed hard and pressed her lips together. When he thought he was going to have to shake the truth out of her, Jodie quietly responded. "Six weeks ago."

He gripped the side of the bed tighter as the white-hot anger spread inside him. *Six weeks.*

The woman had plenty of opportunity to give him the news. She knew he wanted to be informed of any consequences of that night. He had demanded that she add his contact information in her phone. But she had distracted him with a lie that had sent him into a tailspin.

Jodie cautiously glanced up at him when he didn't respond. "I was trying to find the right time," she insisted. "The right words."

"Or were you stalling because you were considering other options? Like getting rid of the child and never telling me."

"No! I wouldn't do that!" She wrapped her arms over her stomach. "I wasn't planning to have this baby but I want it."

His eyes narrowed on her protective gesture. Why was she trying to protect the baby from him? The rage flashed through him, burning hot and destructive, and it hurt to breathe. "Why did you tell me you were pregnant in September?"

Jodie's cheeks turned pink and she slowly lifted her hands as if to placate him. "You have to understand."

"Do you think I'm going to show you mercy because you're pregnant?" His low voice shook as he struggled to remain icy calm. "You had planned to keep my baby from me. It's as good as stealing my child."

"No!" Jodie's eyes filled with tears as if she'd been struck.

"You weren't going to tell me." He drew in a shallow breath as the fury billowed inside him. He often expected the worst in people, but he was stunned by Jodie's treachery. "You were going to let me believe another man was the father."

"No, not exactly." She pressed the heels of her hand against her forehead.

"Trying to keep all your lies straight?"

She slapped her hands on the mattress. "I lied to you when I said I was pregnant. I didn't know I was actually going to have a baby."

Stergios leaned forward, his face inches away from hers as he bared his teeth. "Why did you tell me you were pregnant with another man's child?"

"I knew that we had started up something. It was a sexual obsession that could keep us from what we really wanted. I knew if I told that lie you wouldn't forgive me. You could cast me out of your life and both of us could move on."

Stergios pushed away from the bed. It sickened

him that Jodie, of all people, knew how he would react. She had used her intimate knowledge of him against him. "All this time I wondered why you singled me out and told me."

"Listen to me, Stergios," she pleaded.

"I don't want to hear any more lies," he said as he turned away.

"Are you and Aleka engaged?"

He froze and his back went straight. No one knew about those plans. What did Jodie know and how was she going to use it against him? "How do you know about that?"

She dismissed his question with the wave of her hand. "My father mentioned that when he visited me in October. Yes or no, Stergios. Are you engaged?"

"*Oxi.* No." They were finalizing the deal and he would formally ask Aleka in the New Year. He dipped his head. Those plans were ruined. His family would not strengthen their power base because he had to marry the mother of his child. "This does not explain why you lied. Why you were hiding my child from me!"

She took a deep breath. "I thought I was doing you a favor."

"A favor?" The rage pressed against his skin, ready to burst free. "Denying me my child is a favor?"

"We're a burden to you." Her voice cracked as if it hurt to say the words out loud. "You are marrying someone else so you can get everything you want in life."

"Not anymore." Having a baby changed everything. "This child is mine and I want him to know his father."

Only Stergios didn't know the first thing about being a father. His pulse raced at the idea that there was a baby relying on him. He had always known that once he had children, he would be nothing like his father. Now the time had come and he was scared that he would be just like Elias Pagonis. They shared the same blood and the same mannerisms. Hell, he even looked like his father.

His stomach churned. "I'm going to be part of this child's life," he said in a low, harsh tone. "I'm giving him the protection of my name and I'm going to guide him through every milestone. Do not assume that I have no interest in becoming a father."

"I know I am the last woman you'd want to carry your child," she retorted.

He clenched his jaw. "That's not true."

"I remember what you said on the island."

He rubbed his hands over his face, regretting those words of anger. *I'm grateful that my child wouldn't have you for a mother. A whore, a liar and an outcast.* At the time he had meant them. He had said those words to wound, to make Jodie suffer with him.

"You are the mother of my child and how I feel about you is irrelevant," he said coldly as he pushed back the memory of the lancing pain her lies had caused. "All that matters is that we get married."

Her mouth twisted with defiance. "No."

Stergios began to pace around the suite. She would come around. Once she realized all he had to offer to her and the child, she would grab at the engagement ring. He would be the one who had much to lose. The marriage to Jodie would cause a scandal. She was his stepsister and a woman who had encouraged a questionable reputation.

The Diamantopoulos family would be furious and humiliated no matter how much diplomacy and tact he used. They had been important friends of the family and would have been good allies. Now they would become powerful enemies.

"You're not listening to me." Jodie's voice filtered into his troubled thoughts.

And he would have a war on his hands with his board of directors. When news of his hasty wedding and unsuitable bride came out, it would reflect poorly on him and the Antoniou Group.

"Stergios!" Her frustrated tone rang in the suite. "We don't need to get married."

He gradually turned around and glared at Jodie. She should be grateful that he was accepting his responsibility. "We do and we will."

"Let me rephrase it." She flattened her hands against her chest. "*I* don't need to get married. I have my money, a place of my own and the ability to give this child every opportunity."

"This is the heir to the Antoniou fortune," he declared as he thrust his hands in the air. "We have to get married."

"No one needs to know, especially if I live in America and—"

He jerked his head back. “You are going to deny me access to my child.”

She blinked hard. “No, we can come to an agreement before the baby is born.”

“Fight for custody?” His skin went cold. “You know that I was a pawn in a custody battle between my parents. You know what happened to me and to my family. And now you want me to relive it?”

Her eyes widened. “Stergios, that’s not what I said.”

He had to get out of here before he said or did something he would regret. “I will not beg for a chance to see my child,” he said gruffly as he strode to the door.

“You cannot force me into marriage,” she called after him.

“For years I have gathered wealth and power to protect my family.” He turned around and captured her gaze. When she paled, he knew his eyes shone with bloodlust. “I have made choices that an honorable gentleman wouldn’t just to keep them safe. You will soon discover that I will use every weapon at my disposal to take care of my child.”

* * *

Jodie stared listlessly out the window while she lay in bed. She paid little attention to the glorious view of Athens. Her head still ached from her restless night. She had wept until she had succumbed to a fitful sleep.

Stergios had every right to be angry with her. To hate her. She had lied to him, held back information and created a mess in his life. She knew he was ruthless enough to take her baby. He didn't play fair and he would cut her out of the baby's life if he thought she was a threat. She didn't have the power to fight him.

Jodie tensed when she felt as though she was being watched. Studied. Analyzed. She cast a covert glance at the door and her muscles locked when she saw Stergios standing at the threshold. Her pulse began to gallop. The man looked formidable in his dark gray suit and red tie. She was not ready for another onslaught.

"I haven't been discharged by the doctor," she told him.

"I want to apologize about last night," he said stiffly as he clasped his hands behind his back. "I had just been informed that I was going to be a father and my emotions got the best of me. I didn't mean to make those threats."

She knew that wasn't true. Stergios had meant every word. In any other circumstance, he would have kept his thoughts to himself. But the idea of becoming a father had paralyzed him. He was scared that he was going to live through his childhood nightmare.

That was why he wanted an obedient wife, Jodie decided as she studied his carefully blank expression. It was also why he pushed himself to inhuman lengths to amass incredible wealth and power. He needed to protect and rely on himself so he didn't have to trust anyone else.

And he had no reason to trust her. She had lied to him, for him, so many times. That ended now. He may never trust her again but he deserved her honesty. "I'm sorry that you found out this way," she said. "I wish I could make it up to you."

"There is something you can do," he said softly as he entered the room.

Alarm sprinted down her spine. She should have known Stergios would play on her guilt and immediately launch into negotiations. "I'm not marrying you because I'm pregnant."

He shook his head and stepped closer to her bed. "I want you to stay in Greece."

His request took her by surprise. Wouldn't he want to hide her away from his colleagues and family? "For how long?"

Stergios gripped the side of her bed, his knuckles white with tension. "I want the baby to be born here. It's very important to me."

She knew that was an understatement and she wondered why he was downplaying it. Stergios was proud of his heritage and would want to share every aspect of it with his child. She wanted her baby to recognize his home and have an unbreakable sense of belonging. To find comfort in traditions and rituals handed down from his father.

But where would that leave her? This wasn't where she belonged. She had constantly been reminded that this was not her home or her family. If she granted Stergios's request, was it the first step to make her an outsider in her baby's life?

"My…my life is in New York." That was where her friends lived. They were her support system.

"I know that I'm asking a lot." His eyes were watchful as though he could read her every thought. "But if you stay here, I can attend the doctor's visits. I can be part of the pregnancy."

An image wavered in front of her. She saw Stergios's hand curved along her pregnant stomach. His touch was possessive and tender and his eyes were wide with wonder. He shared one of those special smiles with her as their baby kicked against his hand.

She blinked hard and the image disappeared. Jodie shifted against her pillow as she tried to ease the jittery feeling. Why had she imagined that? It was pure fantasy. She shouldn't make a decision based on a dream. "You won't have time to be part of it."

"I will make the time," he promised.

Jodie scoffed at that statement. "I've heard all the excuses before. My mother was obsessed with work just like you. Any family commitments were the first to be broken."

He leaned down, holding her gaze with his. "You need to give me a chance," he insisted in a low, urgent tone.

She knew he was right. It was only fair. He might prove to be an excellent father. The man protected his family and demonstrated loyalty, responsibility and care. He would extend that to his child.

But what about her? Was that why she was afraid to give him a chance? She knew she was being selfish but it was a genuine concern. What if she started to rely on him and he failed her? What if he got bored with the idea of being a father after she made room in her life for him?

She had to take the risk. Her heart beat loudly against her chest wall. She had been pushing people away before they had a chance to discard her. She had to give Stergios a chance. She wanted her baby to have a father he could rely on. That had to start now.

"Okay, Stergios. I will stay in Greece. Just until the baby is born," she added.

Her stomach twisted when she saw the triumph gleam in his eyes before he quickly banked it. The man who promised to care for her and for her baby might be her greatest protector. So why did her instincts tell her that she'd just stepped into a trap?

CHAPTER ELEVEN

JODIE WAS UNNATURALLY silent when they returned to the Antoniou estate later that day. She was deep in thought when he helped her out of her winter coat. He noticed that her brown printed dress and low heels mirrored her subdued nature.

"Is my mother here?" he asked the butler as he gave him the coats.

"She and Kyrios Little are waiting for you in the salon." The butler gave Jodie a commiserating look before he gave a small bow.

They walked into the entrance hall and Jodie hung back, her gaze locked onto the Christmas tree. "I think it would be best if I found my own place in Athens. It wouldn't be right if I stay here."

"They know, *pethi mou*." Stergios curled his arm around her waist. He felt the shock reverberating inside her. "I have informed our parents that you are pregnant."

"You didn't have that right!" she whispered fiercely.

"I have every right." Stergios forcefully bit out the words. "The child is mine."

Jodie's shoulders slumped. "Did you tell them that, as well?"

"Of course. I am not going to hide it."

She closed her eyes as she rubbed her fingertips against her forehead. Jodie appeared pale and Stergios wondered if she should have stayed in the hospital for one more day.

"I can't walk in there," she confessed. "It's going to be a feeding frenzy."

"I won't let that happen," Stergios said as he guided her with his hand splayed possessively against the curve of her hip. "I will take the brunt of it."

"I don't want that, either," she explained. "And you don't have to worry about me. I'm not going to break into pieces because someone thinks I'm a whore."

His mouth pinched. "Don't say that."

"Why?" she asked, walking stiffly to the salon. "You used that word to describe me."

He had and he was not proud of it. "You wanted

me to think you were when you made claims of another man, but that is no excuse. I shouldn't have and I won't let anyone else treat you with disrespect."

Jodie pressed her lips together but she didn't argue. "Tell me what I should expect before I walk into the lion's den. How did your mother take the news?" She gave him a knowing look when he hesitated. "You can tell me the truth."

No, he couldn't. Stergios needed to protect Jodie from the vitriol that had spewed from his mother's mouth. "She wants a paternity test as soon as possible."

Jodie nodded. She paused and frowned, her forehead wrinkling. "Why haven't you required it?"

He didn't know why that hadn't been his first priority. It was unlike him. He knew not to trust people until he had absolute proof. Why had he automatically accepted that this child was his when Jodie had lied to him in the past? "The timing fits."

"I know what kind of reputation I have around here but—"

He stopped and cornered her against the carved limestone wall. "Don't."

Jodie straightened to her full height and jutted her chin out. "Don't what?"

"Don't remind me." Stergios curled his finger under her chin and brushed the pad of his thumb against her red lips as if he could wipe away the touch of the other men in her past.

"What I was trying to tell you is that I can take a paternity test but it's not necessary," she said as she pushed his hand away. "I haven't been with a man for a very long time."

Satisfaction rolled through Stergios and he knew she spoke the truth. There had been something in the way she'd touched him during that night. As if she had denied herself for so long and had finally broken free. He rested his forehead against hers as he looked deeply into Jodie's blue eyes. "I was determined to keep you away from Dimos but it wasn't necessary. You were only interested in me. It's always been that way."

She flushed as she scowled at him. "It won't be if you keep gloating about it."

He smiled as he saw the fighting spirit flicker in her eyes. "Come along, *pethi mou*." He offered his hand. “Coffee is about to be served in the salon.”

She ignored his gesture and walked ahead of him. “I’m familiar with the schedule in this house.”

Stergios grabbed her wrist and forced her to a halt. “We’re going into that room as a united front.”

Jodie gave him a sidelong look. “Describe *united*.”

“It means that you aren’t going to fight me, you aren’t going to contradict me and you aren’t going to stir up trouble.” He didn’t want his opposition to notice the cracks in his relationship with Jodie. They would use it and he would lose the ground he had already conquered.

“Don’t do anything that requires me to fight back.” Jodie paused and was clearly considering her next words. “And don’t give them any details about us.”

Stergios tilted his head to one side as he released his hold on her. “I’m not one to confide in others.”

“No one needs to know that you—” her hands churned as she struggled for the right word

"—*detained* me at the island. And they certainly don't need to know what happened four years ago."

"I have no intentions of advertising my lack of judgment. I thought you would at the first opportunity."

Her blue eyes went dull. "Then you don't know me at all."

"Enough of this." He grabbed her hand, lacing his fingers with hers before he led her to the salon. Jodie tried to get out of his grasp.

"United front, Jodie," he reminded her softly.

"That doesn't mean we have to be arm in arm," she said in a hiss.

He gave her hand a squeeze. "You like touching me," he said with a teasing smile. "You definitely like it when I touch you."

"All the more reason not to touch me."

He noticed she didn't deny it, but he also knew she was correct. Stergios couldn't afford any distractions. He reluctantly let go of her hand as they approached the salon but he couldn't break all contact. She needed to know that he was at her side. Placing his hand at the small of her back, he escorted her into the salon.

Stergios immediately saw his mother and Gregory sitting by the fireplace. Tension pulsed in the small, ornate room. He glanced at Jodie as she stood in front of him. He realized she was poised to defend them both. Did she think he wouldn't look after her? Stergios tamped down his displeasure. Jodie needed to trust him.

"Jodie," Gregory said as he rose from his seat and clasped his hands behind his back. "How are you feeling?"

"Better, thank you." Her voice was barely above a whisper.

Stergios noticed that Gregory did not approach his daughter. Jodie immediately took a seat as if she'd known her father's question was out of politeness instead of concern. Stergios had always been aware the two were not demonstrative but it bothered him that Jodie couldn't expect any moral support from her parent.

"The doctor recommended a lot of rest," Stergios said, standing behind Jodie's chair. "More food and liquids."

"And when will it be safe to travel?" Mairi asked.

Stergios recognized the hint of steel underneath

his mother's concerned tone. She was already planning Jodie's return flight. "Jodie is staying in Athens for the duration of her pregnancy."

"Why?" Gregory asked. "Her presence will create a scandal."

"I'm aware of that." Stergios gave his stepfather a disapproving look. He should have known Gregory had no sense of anticipation over his grandchild.

"You need to think about this, Stergios." His mother agitatedly twisted her pearl necklace between her fingers. "The Diamantopoulos family are great friends but they have certain expectations for a future son-in-law. They won't tolerate the fact that you have a love child. We need to keep this secret and get Jodie out of here as soon as possible."

He sensed Jodie's tension soar. Did she think he was going to change his mind? Abandon her and their child? "I no longer have plans to marry Aleka," Stergios announced.

Mairi blanched at the news. "Of course you are," she replied in a brittle voice. "Stergios, think of your duty."

"I am." He placed his hand on Jodie's shoulder. "My duty is to Jodie and our child."

Jodie shifted uncomfortably as the room went silent. She seemed fascinated by the faded rug at her feet, but he knew she was not oblivious to the looks of condemnation.

"This merger must happen," Mairi said as she pulled her attention back onto Stergios. "It will give us unlimited power and influence. We are at the final stages of the agreement. There's no turning back."

"Plans change," Stergios said. He was not going to apologize for this decision. He turned to his stepfather. "And, Gregory, I ask for permission to marry your daughter."

Jodie gasped and twisted around to face him. "Stergios!"

He didn't look at Jodie. He watched Gregory squirm as the panic lit his eyes. He didn't need the man's approval, but had been curious to see how his stepfather would respond. The man would not support Stergios's plans of marriage, but neither would he interfere.

Jodie bolted from her seat and pointed accusingly at him. "We have discussed this and I am not marrying you."

"Oh, thank God," his mother muttered with relief.

Stergios saw Jodie turn pale and she wobbled on her feet. "Excuse me," she said, reaching for him. "I'm not feeling well."

He was at her side and silently encouraged her to lean against him. "What's wrong?"

"I stood up too fast." Jodie closed her eyes. "I'm just going to go lie down."

Stergios lifted her in his arms. She felt delicate against him. When Jodie rested her head against his shoulder and sighed, her display of trust and acceptance nearly undid him. He strode out of the salon, ignoring Gregory's blustering and Mairi's cold silence.

"Put me down, Stergios," she ordered when he stepped into the entrance hall. She winced when she saw the butler carrying the coffee service. The older man stopped to gawk at them. "I don't need for us to make a scene."

"Are you really feeling ill?" he asked.

"Why would I lie?"

He held her closer as he carried her up the

grand staircase. "To save your father from making a choice."

She looked surprised by his insight. "That's why I interrupted. And you shouldn't have asked him that. What happened to the united front you wanted? Anyway, it doesn't matter what my father would have said. We are not getting married."

"Hush," he said gently as he reached the second floor and turned to the right. "You're unwell. You don't know what you're saying."

"I am pregnant, not an invalid. Just because I disagree with you does not make my opinion unsound." Jodie glanced around the hallway. "Where are you taking me?"

"To my room. It's closer."

Stergios's suite of rooms was not what she had expected. The colors of sand and stone from the sitting room were a blur as he carried her to the adjoining bedroom. The furniture's strong lines and natural wood reminded her of his island getaway. It was nothing like the formality of the rest of the house.

He carefully placed her onto his bed and her

pulse skipped a beat. She shouldn't be alone with Stergios. She wouldn't be able to keep her hands off him and it would give him the wrong idea. He would think she was ready to reestablish their relationship.

That couldn't happen. She still wasn't able to give him the life he wanted and he… Her thoughts faded as she watched him remove her shoes. She was so much in love with Stergios that it hurt but he would never love her back. She couldn't take the risk of believing that one day he would reciprocate her feelings.

"I'm going to have your things moved in here," Stergios said as he sat on the edge of the bed.

She bolted up into a sitting position. "Have you lost your mind?" The room tilted and she groaned.

"Lie down." He grasped her shoulders and lowered her onto the mattress.

"I'm serious, Stergios," she said as she laid her head on the pillow. "I am not sharing a room with you. I will find a place of my own. In the meantime, I will stay in a hotel."

"Wherever you go, I go."

She peeked at him from under her lashes. When

she saw his determined look and the clench of his jaw she knew she had a battle on her hands. "I said I would stay in Greece. I didn't say I would stay with you."

He stroked her hair away from her face. "You need someone to look after you."

She couldn't argue that after he had caught her from fainting and carried her to the nearest bed. "I'll hire someone."

Stergios tucked a strand of hair behind her ear. "*Oxi*, I want to be part of this pregnancy."

She rose up and rested against her elbows. "And what will happen if we get married and I have the child? What becomes of me?"

He caressed the length of her throat with the back of his hand as he frowned. "What do you mean?"

Jodie bit down on her tongue. She hadn't planned to voice those concerns but now they were out in the open. "You only want to get married so you have a legal claim on your baby. What happens next?"

"We raise our child."

"Together? I doubt that." She may not be part of Stergios's social stratosphere, but she knew what happened when women married powerful men. "I'm going to be pushed off to the side. I'll be the outsider. You'll send me away and keep the baby."

He gave her an odd, slanted smile. "I won't."

"And it would only be a matter of time before you and the baby forget about me."

"Impossible," he said as his hands rested on the mattress. His arms bracketed her and he lowered his head. "I want our child to have many brothers and sisters."

Hope was a dangerous thing, Jodie thought as a lump formed in her throat. "What?"

"I've never liked being an only child." Stergios pressed his mouth against her cheek. "I know you haven't, either."

She wanted a big family. She had often dreamed of a home that was bursting at the seams with children, laughter and love.

Stergios left a trail of soft kisses along her jaw. "A marriage is meant to protect your property and heirs. I will make you my wife if it means protecting my family but I have no interest in a paper marriage," he said. "Once we marry, you will share my bed and have my children."

His gentle, soothing tone couldn't hide the fierceness behind his words. "How can you make a declaration like that?" she asked as she lay back down. "We aren't even in a relationship."

Stergios hovered above her and she saw the possessive gleam in his eye. "That needs to change immediately."

"Stop." Her heart pounded wildly as she pressed her fingertips against his mouth. "You can't seduce me into marriage."

The challenge flickered in his eyes and she held her breath. What was she doing throwing down the gauntlet like that? She knew she would promise him anything if it meant one more kiss, one more touch.

"I wouldn't dream of it," he said as he captured her hand and kissed her fingertips. "Now go to sleep. You need your rest."

She snatched her hand away. "I mean it, Stergios. I won't live with you and I won't share a bed."

"*Ne*, you will, *pethi mou*. Very soon," he promised as he stood up. "You will give me everything I want and more."

CHAPTER TWELVE

"ARE YOU SURE you want to do this?" Jodie whispered to Stergios as they walked through the cavernous museum to the Antoniou collection. Her black ball gown swished against her legs as they followed the colorful banners that announced the highly anticipated display.

"I have been looking forward to this event," Stergios said as they entered the archway that led to the exclusive party. "The Antoniou family donated historically important artifacts to the museum and it will be on tour for years."

"No, that's not what I meant. I know you want to be here." The pride had shimmered from him as they had entered the prestigious building and she didn't want to do anything to diminish it. "Are you sure you want me to attend. With you?"

He stopped and studied her strained smile. "You're nervous," he said in disbelief.

Of course she was nervous! She didn't want to

let him down. Her spine grew rigid when she felt all eyes on her. Jodie swept her gaze along the crowd. They appeared reticent but at least they weren't hostile.

Stergios splayed his hand against her back. The casual touch did little to calm her nerves. She still slept in a separate room. There were some nights when she wished she hadn't drawn a line on their relationship. She was frequently tempted to move into his room and stake her claim but something held her back. She still wasn't sure if Stergios's solicitude was temporary or an attempt to lower her guard.

It didn't help that he was wearing a black tuxedo that accentuated his lean, masculine body. Her mouth had gone dry and a wicked curl of heat had settled low in her pelvis when she had first seen him. His knowing smile had irked her but she still had difficulty dragging her gaze away.

"Just be yourself," he said as he brushed his mouth against her ear. "Stay close to me if you're feeling uncertain."

She gave a choked laugh. "Okay, that's not the advice I usually get." It was usually keep her mouth shut and make herself scarce.

"Why did you want me to attend?" she asked. She felt like she was a curiosity and her presence would detract from the display.

He nodded at someone in the crowd. Everyone seemed to know him but they were too intimidated to draw near. "It's an event that honors my family's history."

"I'm not family. We are not engaged and I'm not marrying you." She was compelled to remind him. During the past few weeks she got the feeling that Stergios was playing a waiting game and believed it was only a matter of time before she acquiesced.

"But you are carrying my child." He lifted her hand and pressed his mouth against her knuckles before he tucked her hand against his elbow. "I want everyone to know that you are under my protection. When your pregnancy is announced, they will know that I claim my child."

"Wouldn't it be better protection if you kept quiet about us?" she asked as she looked around the room and found everyone was openly staring at them. "No one has to know."

He drew his head back and he studied her

through hooded eyes. “Are you ashamed that I got you pregnant?”

“No!” She was stunned that he would think that. She wanted Stergios’s baby and couldn’t imagine sharing this bond with any other man.

His heated gaze drifted down her plunging neckline and leisurely traveled back up until it rested on her necklace. “Is it strange that I want to show you off?”

“Yes!” She looked away when he laughed and she fiddled with her earring.

Jodie immediately put her hand down. She didn’t want to damage the jewelry. When Stergios had presented the amethyst earrings and necklace in an old wooden box she knew they were heirlooms. At first she had declined wearing something of such sentimental value but Stergios had insisted.

Brushing her hand along the necklace as if she wanted to make sure it was still there, Jodie couldn’t help but stand a little taller while she wore the jewels. Stergios’s gesture had honored her. She didn’t want to look too deeply into what it meant or whether he’d have allowed her to wear them if she wasn’t carrying his child.

"My security team recommended I keep quiet about you," he admitted.

"And you disregarded their suggestion?" Stergios had been very protective of her since she had returned from the hospital. His gestures often left her flustered or inordinately touched. "This event must mean a lot to you."

"In fact, they wish you were inside the Antoniou estate right now so no harm will come to you," he said as a waiter approached them with a tray of drinks.

"And your family wished I was home so I wouldn't cause any trouble." She gave a squeeze to his arm. "Don't worry, I wouldn't do anything to embarrass you."

"I know you won't. Your past antics were designed to be noticed," he said as he reached for a flute of orange juice and handed it to her. "You didn't want to be forgotten or ignored. You don't have to do that anymore. You have my full attention."

She felt the heat flood her chest and crawl up her neck. She looked away before it flooded her cheeks. Jodie's hectic gaze collided with a familiar pair of brown eyes. She felt the bands of tension release from her rib cage when she saw the friendly face. "There are many people here who will remember my past," she said with a wide smile.

"Recognize anyone?"

"Yes, one of the benefits of attending so many schools around the world is that I probably know someone at any high-society events." She nodded to the brunette who waved excitedly at her. "There is Sofia Xenakis. I haven't seen her since I got kicked out of our boarding school. We never had a chance to meet whenever I was in Athens."

"Is her father Theodoros Xenakis? The media mogul?"

She heard the rare hitch of curiosity in his voice. "Yes, do you know him?"

"Of him," he corrected with a grimace. "I've wanted a meeting with him for years but he's a recluse. He doesn't meet with anyone outside his inner circle."

"Is that so?" She hid her smile against the fluted glass. She may not be part of Athens high society but that didn't make her an impediment for Stergios and his business activities.

His eyes narrowed with suspicion. "Yes, why?"

Her smile grew so wide that her cheeks hurt. "I've been to his house in the Bahamas several times during school vacations. He's a sweetie. Come with me and I'll introduce you to his daughter."

Stergios leaned against the stone museum wall as he typed on his cell phone, replying to an urgent message. He didn't notice his cousin approaching until the man stood next to him. "Dimos," he said by way of greeting. "I didn't know you were attending. Is Zoi here, too?"

"I don't have to be joined at the hip with my wife," Dimos said with a scowl before he pointed accusingly at the center of the room. "What is she doing here?"

"Jodie is my guest for the evening," he said as he pocketed his cell phone.

"Why?" Dimos broadly gestured at the crowd. "There are too many photographers and journalists here. You're supposed to be courting the Diamantopoulos heiress."

Stergios tried to remember what Aleka Diamantopoulos looked like. It had only been a couple of weeks since he had been pursuing the woman. He had found her docile and ultimately forgettable. He knew Aleka had been raised to marry a powerful man but it had taken a great deal of patience and energy to tamp down his natural aggression when she was around. He couldn't show his true self or it would have frightened her.

Unlike Jodie, he thought as he watched her tilt her head back and give a bawdy laugh that rang in the pretentious museum. The woman had seen him at his worst and she didn't walk away. She wasn't afraid to disagree with him or prove him wrong. Jodie was also under the misguided impression that she needed to protect him. It was during those moments when she'd unwittingly displayed her loyalty.

Dimos winced as everyone looked at Jodie. "The Diamantopoulos family isn't going to be happy that you brought another woman to this important event, even if it is your stepsister. They want to see you pander to their daughter. It's a power play."

"I am no longer pursuing the Antoniou-Diamantopoulos merger." It was strange that he felt no regret. The alliance would have given him everything he wanted. But now his focus was on marrying Jodie. That pursuit filled him with anticipation.

Dimos's shoulders slumped as he gave a sigh of disappointment. "Because you got Jodie pregnant?"

Stergios swung his head around in shock. How did Dimos know about that? Jodie wouldn't divulge that kind of information. He studied his cousin and was immediately on guard. He didn't like the flint of bitterness and envy flashing in the man's eyes.

"Yes, I've heard," Dimos said bluntly. "Your mother is trying to keep the rumors from spreading. It's no use. People are going to find out."

"Good." He had a strategy in place to present Jodie to society in the best light.

"Good?" Dimos repeated before he took a fortifying sip of his drink. "How can you say that? I don't know why you're taking a public stand on this. You know, you're not the first Antoniou man who has had children outside of marriage."

Stergios arched an eyebrow. "Is there something I should know, Dimos?"

His cousin waved away the question. "You don't have to throw out everything we've worked hard for just to acknowledge a child. There is no need to give the kid your name. Why support it when Jodie has money of her own?"

"You wouldn't understand." He would protect his heir even if it meant extending that protection to the mother of his child.

Dimos finished his drink in one gulp as he watched Jodie talk animatedly while she stood among a few socialites. "Oh, hell, no," he said in a low tone as his eyes widened. "Jodie is wearing the Antoniou amethysts?"

Stergios nodded with satisfaction as he watched the violet stones twinkle from her ears and throat. Jodie was made to wear the amethysts.

"Well, there's no hiding it now." His cousin raised his hands in defeat. "No wonder all of high society is flocking around Jodie. Even the reporters will know what this means. You are telling everyone that she will be an Antoniou."

But Jodie didn't know that the jewelry was more than heirlooms. One day he would tell her that the stones were part of family legend and ritual. When he had draped the necklace around her slender throat, he had been declaring Jodie as his intended bride. He claimed Jodie as his own and now everyone knew that she was his.

"Does your mother know that woman is wearing the jewels?"

"Show some respect," Stergios warned in a growl. "*That woman* is going to be my wife and the mother of my child."

"Why are you doing this?" Dimos asked in a hiss. "Is she so good in bed that she's twisted your mind?"

"You'll never know. Is that what's eating you up?"

Dimos cast a vicious glare. "Even I knew as a teenager that Jodie isn't the type of woman you marry," he said. "She's the disposable lover. Try her once or twice and then discard—"

Hot fury flashed through Stergios and he grabbed Dimos by the tie. "Don't."

Dimos grappled at Stergios's hand. "Let go of me," he said weakly, glancing at the interested spectators around them. "People are watching."

"I don't care," he said through clenched teeth.

"I'm not saying anything that hasn't been said before," he choked as his face turned bright red.

"That's going to change," Stergios announced as he let go of his cousin.

Dimos coughed as he loosened his tie. "Are you going to threaten every relative? You'll be popular at the next family dinner."

He didn't need to be liked. He needed Jodie happy and content living in Greece. "I will do whatever is necessary for Jodie to be accepted."

"That's never going to happen," his cousin predicted as he took a cautious step back. "You are going to be the laughingstock of all of Athens if you marry a woman like that. They will shun her."

"Then give them a message from me," he said in a chilling tone. "If you disrespect Jodie, you disrespect me. Hurt her in any way and I will come after you. Got that?"

"You're making a big mistake," Dimos said as he slunk away. "But you'll figure that out soon enough. I just hope you don't take the Antoniou family down with you."

CHAPTER THIRTEEN

A WEEK LATER Stergios cautiously approached Jodie's bedroom as he planned his next move. He felt like he was flying without a net. What he said or did next could ruin all of the groundwork he'd covered so far.

The door to her room was ajar. There was a clatter of something hitting the floor and Jodie's muttered expletive followed. Stergios tapped his knuckles on the door before he pushed it open.

His eyes lit up with appreciation when he saw Jodie. Her lime-green tank top and charcoal-gray yoga pants clung to her curves. She was stretching, extending her arm as she reached for something at the top of her closet. Wisps of her blond hair were escaping from her short ponytail. It took him a moment to notice the open suitcase on her bed.

His chest tightened. "What is this?" he asked in a low, dangerous tone.

Jodie jumped at the sound of his voice and whirled around. Her face was red with exertion and her eyes gleamed with anger. He suspected she could tear up at any moment.

"What does it look like?" she asked defiantly as she bundled up a dress and tossed it in the case. "I'm leaving."

Panic flared deep inside him. Suddenly he was at her side and grasped her arm to stop her. "No, you're not."

"I have to," she insisted as she shook off his hold. "I swore I wasn't going to live like this again."

"What happened?" He was glad he had followed his instinct and had arrived home early. He couldn't afford the time off but he had felt his relatives' seething anger just under the surface in the breakfast room this morning. He knew the Antonious resented Jodie's presence but he couldn't tell how it affected her.

This was his fault. He had not expected his family to question his choices. They hadn't before but now they felt Jodie had seduced him down a different path. A mutiny was brewing. A week ago he couldn't have imagined any of the

Antonious dissecting his decisions. They used to congregate around him like devoted servants wanting to please their master.

Stergios never took their obsequious manner as his due. He knew they only wanted his advice, his help and his money. He had often found it irritating. Maybe that was why he found Jodie's attitude a refreshing challenge.

"I know I'm a burden, just like I was when I was a teenager." Jodie placed her hands on her hips and looked away. "My father is embarrassed by me and he's worried that he's going to be penalized just by being related to me. And Mairi wants me out. Out of the house, the city and their lives. Sound familiar?"

It did. He had thought it would be different this time around. She had him as her ally, her protector. But he was not at home enough to be a physical barrier between Jodie and his family.

"And how do I respond to all this? I'm hiding again." She angrily tossed a pair of shoes into the suitcase. "That had been my strategy when I first came to live here. Then I did the opposite only to find more grief. I'm trying to become invisible because this family refuses to make room for me."

Stergios reached for the suitcase and flipped the lid closed. "You made a promise and I expect you to keep it."

"You made promises to me, as well. You said you would make time for the baby and me. Instead you spend every waking moment at the office." She returned to the closet and snagged a dress off the hanger. "My mother used to do that when she was building an empire of her own. I was alone then and I'm alone now."

"It won't be like this at the office for much longer," he said. He would be home in the evenings once he had taken care of the public relations nightmare. News of getting his stepsister pregnant should have been a six-day wonder, but it didn't help that there was no forthcoming wedding date. It showed his lack of commitment to the mother of his child. It suggested instability in the Antoniou family, not to mention legal ambiguity for his heir.

"I feel trapped," she admitted. "I swore I wasn't going to live like this again and I immediately fall into my old patterns. I stay in my room and out of the way or I'm in the garden."

"You are not leaving."

"I'm staying in Greece. Just not here in this house. I'm moving into a hotel for the short term." She smoothed her hands over her hair and gave a deep sigh. "I should have done it from the beginning. Why did you want me to stay here?"

"This is the safest place for you," he explained. "We have the best security here and no one can get to you."

Jodie lifted her gaze to the ceiling as if she was saying a heartfelt prayer. "You don't have to worry, Stergios. I keep telling you that but you don't listen. I promise you that no one is out to get me."

He gritted his teeth before he informed her of the threats his security team started to receive once they made their first appearance at the museum. It was the usual. They wanted to steal from her or hurt her. They wanted to take her from him.

Stergios was used to the threats being aimed at him. After his kidnapping, he learned to expect the worst in humanity. At times it was white noise and he was numbed to it. But when his security team told him about the first threat against Jodie, his rage had been swift and brutal.

"You are now a public figure," he said. He was not going to tell her about the warnings and threats. Jodie should be allowed to live her life without fear.

"I will be safe in a hotel," she promised.

"You will be safer here," he argued.

Jodie paused and crossed her arms. "Are you trying to protect me or are you trying to keep me from finding out about the scandal?"

He lifted his head as the puzzle pieces started to fall into place. That was why she had this sudden need to leave. She discovered that the scandal was weakening him. His family and colleagues were not standing behind him. His enemies had smelled blood and were circling around him.

Stergios wasn't worried. It was an inconvenience more than anything. At least he knew who his true allies were.

"I found out about it today," she said. "I would have earlier but it's been a while since I've seen a newspaper. Oh, and the internet connection has been under repairs for a week." She arched an eyebrow. "What a coincidence."

He rubbed his hand against the back of his neck. How did she find out? "I don't want you to worry about it. The doctor said to avoid stress."

"Avoid stress," she repeated dully. "How can I when I'm the source of it all?"

Stergios stared at her. He didn't see her that way. She might challenge and frustrate him, but she also brought him joy and light. Jodie was his port in the storm swirling around him.

"You've been through so much in your life. You've overcome horrific experiences and you were on to great things..." Jodie's eyes filled with tears. "And then I showed up."

He didn't like the sound of defeat in her voice. "Have a little more faith in my abilities, Jodie," he retorted drily. "I have accomplished many things and I've only just begun."

Jodie wasn't listening. "You should have married Aleka," she said softly.

"That ship has sailed," he said in a growl. He had heard that suggestion from everyone, but lately he felt as if he'd dodged a bullet.

She looked at the window. "Maybe I should go

back to America." She sounded preoccupied as if she was already making plans. "It would be better for both of us."

"*Oxi!* No!" He moved in front of her, blocking her from the suitcase.

She took a step to the side. "Don't worry, I can be back in time for the birth."

He stretched out his arm to stop her. "That is out of the question."

"The baby will be born in Greece, I promise. You can trust me, Stergios."

"Trust?" he spat out. "Unbelievable. Why should I trust you when you won't give me the same courtesy?"

Her eyes went wide. "I don't understand. What are you talking about?"

"You hide how you feel because you don't trust me. You don't tell me what's worrying you. Why? Do you think I can't fix it?" His anger flashed at the possibility. "That I'm going to ignore your concerns?"

"You don't share your concerns with me, either," she pointed out.

Stergios scoffed. That was different. He was concealing information so she would be happy living here. "It is my job to protect you and the baby. Instead of letting me take care of it, you want to walk away."

"That's not how I see it. You are losing everything you worked hard for because of us. Because of me. And you choose not to tell me."

"Because I didn't want you to grab at the excuse and leave." He gestured wildly as hard, cold fear settled in his stomach. "I am not going to lose you and the baby."

Her shoulders sagged and she sat down on the bed. "Why does it matter if I stay?"

It mattered. Stergios raked his hand in his hair as he took a deep breath. He was already losing her. They didn't share the same room or a bed. She was pushing him away and he couldn't let that happen.

He had to make a compromise. It went against every instinct but he knew if he didn't, Jodie would leave him. "I'm going to be wherever you are." The words came out with great reluctance. "If you don't want to stay in this house, then decide where we're going to live."

She was already shaking her head. "You can't

be away from your office. Not now, not when everyone is out for your blood."

Stergios crouched down in front of her. He knew she had some place in mind but she was trying to talk herself out of it. "I will figure something out. Where, Jodie?"

"I want to go back to your home on the island."

He went still. Stergios thought Jodie would associate his home with bad memories. It was where he had kidnapped her, where he had cast her out of his life. "Why there?"

"You're right," she muttered. "It wouldn't work. That's your island getaway. It's not meant for everyday living. It doesn't have a phone line."

"Not anymore." He grasped her hands in his. "After our weekend I made extensive updates on the house. It has the newest technology and a generator that works. But when I found out about the baby, I started making some more changes."

Her face lit up. "Really? You're making room for the baby?" She squeezed his hands. "I want to see. You have to take me there, Stergios. I want to go back to your home as soon as possible."

"Our home," he corrected. "And I'll take you right now."

* * *

Jodie felt a sense of peace once she arrived on the island hours later. She inhaled the scent of the ocean and listened to the rustling leaves. She hadn't felt this calm in weeks. She had been tense and on guard while she was at the Antoniou house, but here she knew she could relax and settle in. Maybe even make this place the home she'd always wanted.

"We're almost done with the renovations for this house," Stergios said as he opened the door. "Don't worry about the construction site that you saw when we flew in. It's on the other side of the island. I'm having them build some cottages for the employees."

"Employees?" she asked. It would feel different sharing this paradise with others.

"We will need a cook and a nanny in addition to the caretaker."

Jodie bit her bottom lip to stop her smile. She was surprised that Stergios had time to think about hiring nannies. She liked his growing anticipation and how he was making room in his life for the baby.

Following Stergios into the house, she watched

him lift her suitcases and carry them into the main room. Anticipation fluttered low in her belly as she watched the play of muscles under his white button-down shirt. Her gaze drifted to his lean waist and powerful thighs.

Jodie darted her gaze away. She ached to touch him. Hold him. But how could she when she had rejected his advances weeks ago? "What renovations did you have done?" she asked as she walked across the main room.

"The most advanced technology and communication features. I'll show you how the touch screens work later."

Jodie walked to the room she had used before. She blinked when she discovered the guest room was empty. There were no furniture or light fixtures. "Stergios?" she called over her shoulder. "What happened to my room?"

"We've only just finished the renovations and updates," he said. "That can be the nursery. You can decorate it any way you want."

She slowly turned around and found him still in the main room, resting his shoulder against a wall. *Do not make a big deal out of this.* "So there's only one bedroom?"

His pose was casual but he watched her intently. "Yes."

She glanced in the direction of his bedroom and was instantly besieged with erotic memories of the last time she stayed there. Jodie cleared her throat. "I should sleep in the main room," she said hoarsely.

"I would never allow a woman to sleep on a sofa."

She knew from the tone of his voice that he would not be swayed. Jodie walked to the sofas that circled the fireplace. "It's not long enough for you to stretch out on." She gestured at the soft white cushions. "And you're barely getting enough sleep as it is. I can't let you sleep there."

"I won't."

Her pulse skipped a beat. Jodie dragged her gaze back to Stergios. If he wasn't staying in the main room, then that meant…

Stergios grabbed his computer tablet from his briefcase and sat down on the sofa. "It's late and you should get some rest. I'm going to get some work done."

Her heart started to race. They were sharing

a bedroom. They were going to share a bed. All night.

She knew she should tell him that under no circumstances were they sharing a room. Instead, Jodie silently grabbed her overnight suitcase and walked to the bedroom with stiff legs. She closed the door and stared at the wide bed. Excitement pulsed inside her.

No, she had nothing to be excited about. Sharing a bed did not mean sex. Even if she was sharing it with the virile Stergios Antoniou. It was not an invitation. She had to remember that. She might want to be intimate and naked with Stergios, but she had made a big mistake when she had refused earlier.

She had told him they weren't resuming their affair because they had no relationship. Instead of arguing, he had granted her wish. He had not made any attempt to get her into bed since.

He was willing to share a bed because he no longer fought the overwhelming need for her. Why? What did she do to kill the attraction? Was it because she was pregnant? Or was it because no woman could hold his interest?

She had to be careful. One word, one move,

and she wouldn't be able to keep her hands off him. Her skin heated as she remembered the last time she claimed him. If she had sex with him again, he would discover exactly how she felt about him. And Stergios would ruthlessly use it to his full advantage.

CHAPTER FOURTEEN

"STERGIOS?"

He heard Jodie from far away. Blackness surrounded him and he tried to kick and claw his way to the surface. He had to get to Jodie. She sounded desperate. Afraid.

"Stergios?" Her sharp voice cut through the last barrier. "Wake up."

He was suddenly awake. His heart pounded against his chest as he took big gulps of air. His eyes burned as he checked his surroundings. He was no longer in the loud and chaotic police station where his family had been irrevocably torn apart. He wasn't the vulnerable child who couldn't bear to be touched or held.

He was safe. No one could hurt him. He wasn't alone anymore. Stergios turned his head to the side and saw Jodie leaning over him.

"What happened?" he asked hoarsely through parched lips. His throat hurt. Everything ached.

"You were shouting." Jodie cupped his face with her hands. Her touch was cool to his skin. She wore a light pink slip and one strap fell from her shoulder. Her hair was tousled from sleep and her concern shimmered from her blue eyes. "Are you okay?"

No, he wasn't. His pulse raced and he was bathed in sweat. "I need a shower," he decided, and bolted from the bed.

"Stergios!"

He rushed to the en suite bathroom as if he were being chased by demons. Once he shut and locked the door behind him, Stergios slumped against the wood and discovered that he was shaking all over.

He ignored Jodie's persistent knocking on the door as he stripped from the black pajama bottoms he had reluctantly put on earlier. Striding naked to the shower, he turned the water on full blast before he stepped in.

Stergios braced his arm against the tile wall as he withstood the cold water. It felt like needles but he didn't move away. He rested his head against his forearm, willing his pulse to slow down and the images to disappear.

He didn't know how long he stayed under the water. He was shivering by the time he stepped out of the shower. He dried his body with rough, brutal strokes.

Wrapping the towel around his waist, Stergios went to the adjoining walk-in closet. He probably had something he would wear to bed. He preferred sleeping in the nude and he was reluctant for anything to touch his skin, but he would do it for Jodie's sake.

Donning on a pair of dark blue pajama bottoms, Stergios took a deep, cleansing breath before he reentered the bedroom. All he had to do was act calm and convince Jodie that everything was fine.

He swung the door open. Just as he had expected, Jodie was blocking his way. Her arms were crossed and she tapped her bare foot on the floor as if she had been waiting there the entire time.

"Are you okay now?" she asked. "How often do you get nightmares?"

"Haven't had them in years." He used to get bad dreams if he had been ill or sleep deprived. During those times, it had been as though his body didn't have the strength to hold back the nightmares.

"What was your dream about?"

"I don't remember." His lie was automatic. He didn't discuss his nightmares. Stergios knew the dreams said more about him and his fears than about the ordeal he had suffered.

He felt her watchful gaze on him as he returned to bed. Jodie quietly got in on her side. He tensed as she lay down, knowing she wasn't going to let the matter drop.

Her proximity set him on edge. The mattress was wide but he was extremely aware of her. Her scent, her warmth, and the sound of the silk slip brushing against the cotton sheets. His willpower had been weakened by the nightmares and he knew he would reach out for her without thinking.

"Are you under a great deal of stress?" she asked. "I know about what's going on in your office. Something about the board of directors losing confidence in your judgment because you accidentally got a woman pregnant. Did I get that right?"

Stergios clenched his jaw. He knew where Jodie

got that information. "And you say my mother never talks to you. No, I'm not concerned about what's going on at the office. Everyone will fall in line and it will be business as usual."

"Then what triggered the nightmare?"

"I haven't been keeping track." Stergios cringed when he recognized his mistake. He sighed and shook his head. There was no stopping Jodie's inquisition now.

She turned toward him. "So there's been more than one. When was the first?"

"The night I left you at the hospital," he answered reluctantly.

Jodie pressed her hand against his hair-roughened chest. "I'm sorry you found out that way. It must have been such a shock."

"I'm fine." He didn't know why he was sticking to that lie when Jodie could feel the rapid thud of his heart.

"Is it the same nightmare?"

"Good night, Jodie. I apologize for waking you up." He turned off the bedside light and tucked his hands under his head. He was exhausted but he knew he wasn't going to get any more sleep.

Jodie reached out and caressed his chest. He

didn't turn away. Stergios needed her soothing touch tonight. The short strokes, back and forth, were surprisingly calming.

"It doesn't matter how I found out about the baby," he eventually said as he stared at the ceiling. "The nightmares would have happened, anyway."

"What do you dream about?" Jodie paused as if she didn't want to encourage more memories. "The kidnappers? The wilderness?"

Exhaustion pulled at his heavy eyelids. *"Oxi,"* he said in a husky voice. "I dream about the day I was rescued."

Jodie's fingers pulled at his curly chest hair. "Why is that a nightmare? Wouldn't that have been a special occasion?"

"It was at first. I was reunited with my family. But my father wasn't there. I had only seen a glimpse of him when I arrived at the police station. And that's when I found out he was the one behind the kidnapping." His voice trailed off as he remembered the overwhelming sense of betrayal.

She continued to stroke his chest. The pattern

was hypnotic and the tension binding his ribs relaxed. He found he could breathe easier.

"He had been arrested and gave up the information as part of a deal," Stergios said bitterly. "He would not tell them anything unless he got something out of it. If he hadn't, I don't know how long I would have been missing."

"And you keep having that bad dream since you discovered you're becoming a father," she murmured. "Have you been dreaming the same thing every night?"

He shook his head. But he had awoken from enough nightmares lately that he was having trouble sleeping. It angered him that he was getting the bad dreams. He thought he was over them, that he had moved to the next level of healing and could get on with his life. Instead, it was as if he had a setback once he'd found out that he was going to be a father.

"Tonight was different," he confessed. Stergios clasped Jodie's hand against his chest. "When I dreamed I had seen a glimpse of him, it wasn't his face. It was mine."

Her fingers flexed, her nails scratching his skin

as the surprise rolled through her. "You are not going to turn out like your father," she whispered.

"You don't know that." He had inherited many traits from Elias Pagonis. He was ruthless and ambitious just like his father.

"I know what kind of man you are, Stergios. I'm well aware of your flaws but you don't have an ounce of evil in you."

A hardened smile tugged at the corner of his mouth. "Don't be too sure."

"I am sure," she retorted. "I'm also certain that your father had made some choices that took him down a path you wouldn't take. Elias Pagonis had to have made some questionable decisions before the kidnapping."

"He was a cheat and a fraud." He had forgotten about Pagonis's other sins. The kidnapping eclipsed everything. With Jodie's prompting, he remembered some of the actions his father had taken. It was as though he'd been building up to kidnapping and extortion. "There were a lot of questions about his finances."

"You are not your father."

At times he was worse. Stergios let go of Jodie's hand. Elias Pagonis had not been the worst man he'd faced. The more power he had accumulated, the more monsters came crawling out, determined to tear him to pieces.

"Your father was a danger to your family," she pointed out, "but you protect them from the likes of Pagonis."

"You don't know my methods." At times he was just as terrifying as the monsters he battled when it meant keeping his loved ones safe.

"You take care of those who are most vulnerable," she continued, stroking the side of his neck. "You will never allow anyone to harm a child."

And it would destroy him if something happened to their child. Or worse, if he shared more than Pagonis's blood. "I can't do this without you," he said gruffly. "You need to let me know if I'm becoming my father."

Her hands froze. "Stergios, it's not going to happen."

"Promise me, Jodie," he pleaded, his voice raw at the edges. He knew he could trust her. She had the courage to tell him when he was wrong and she was the only person who would care about their child as much as he did.

"I promise," she said with great reluctance.

"But you're asking too much of me. I couldn't hurt you like that."

"I'd rather you hurt me than…" The memories started to crowd his mind and he turned away from Jodie. "I can't fail my child."

She pressed her hand against his shoulder. "And that, Stergios," she said softly, "is why you will never be like your father."

Jodie murmured and sighed with contentment as she gradually stirred from her sleep. She was surrounded by heat and wiggled closer. She frowned when she felt Stergios's big hands grasp her arms as the delicious heat faded.

Stergios carefully held her away. "You could tempt a saint, Jodie."

Her eyelashes fluttered as she slowly opened her eyes. "What's wrong?" she asked, her voice groggy from sleep. The bedroom was dark but she saw the first streaks of dawn filter through the curtains.

"You're too close." He growled in her ear. "I knew this would happen if we shared a bed."

Too close? She blinked a few times and discovered that instead of keeping a safe distance, she was clinging onto Stergios. Her head rested against his bare chest as she listened to the solid beat of his heart. She had draped her arms around him in a loose embrace and her hips were flush with his.

At some point in the night she had gravitated to his warmth and strength. She had turned to Stergios in her sleep because she couldn't stay away. Jodie didn't want to hold back anymore. She knew now that Stergios Antoniou wasn't going to hurt her. He cared for her and for the baby.

Jodie unhooked her bare leg from his muscular thigh. His pajama bottoms hung low on his hips and the thin cotton couldn't hide his thick erection. Heat flashed through her pelvis, her core tightening, as she remembered the masculine power he demonstrated when he had thrust inside her.

"Do you want me to go sleep on the sofa?" Her voice sounded strangled as she rolled back onto her side of the bed.

He flung his arm out and caged her. "Try and I'll bring you back here."

"Careful, Stergios," she teased. "You're on my side of the bed."

"This is not a laughing matter, *pethi mou.* Get any closer and I'm going to touch you." His voice thickened. "Take you. And nothing is going to stop me."

"I'll take my chances," she said in a husky purr.

"You didn't want to share a bed, remember?" She shivered when she heard the shaky restraint in his low, masculine voice. "Because we don't have a relationship, you said."

That had been weeks ago when all they shared was the knowledge that they were going to be parents. She had wanted more from Stergios. Some indication that she was more to him than the mother of his child. Now they were taking the first steps together toward a new life.

"But if you think we're going to have a sexless marriage," he said in a rough tone, "then you are out of your mind."

She felt the flicker of a smile on her mouth. "I thought your interest was fading because I wasn't going to be an easy conquest and just tumble into your bed."

"Fading?" He repeated the word in a choked

voice. "Every day I want you more but I don't trust myself around you. I have been in agony all these weeks."

"You hide it well." She curled into him and pressed her mouth against his throat.

She felt him swallow hard as the tension vibrated from his clenched muscles. "Jodie, if I touch you, I won't be gentle."

"The doctors have said it was safe," she reminded him as she curled the tip of her tongue against his skin. "You heard them yourself."

"They don't know how I am around you." His voice wavered.

"But I know you will keep me safe." She arched her spine, pressing her breasts against him. "You will make me ache, Stergios, and you will take me to the edge of pleasure. You will make me surrender until I scream your name, but you will never hurt me."

CHAPTER FIFTEEN

THE ATMOSPHERE CRACKLED between them and Jodie thought he would pounce. That was what she wanted. She needed to feel the lust that was coursing through his veins and colliding with the hard masculine aggression. But Stergios took her by surprise when he claimed her lips with a slow, wet kiss. She moaned as he explored her mouth with the wicked flick of his tongue.

Jodie couldn't contain the growing need pulsating inside her. She caressed his strong body, her touch urgent and greedy. She liked how Stergios's muscles bunched as her fingers swept along his washboard abs. He hissed as her nails raked along his bare back. It was only when she slid her fingertips beneath his waistband that Stergios broke the deeply seductive kiss. She watched the sinful glow of his eyes as she clenched his buttocks.

Stergios's movements were lightning-fast as

he grasped her wrists. He held her hands above her head, her fingers knocking against the wood headboard. Excitement tore at her chest as Stergios pinned her to the mattress.

His grasp was firm as he hovered above her. She lifted her head to kiss him but he would not allow it. She whimpered with frustration as she struggled to break free.

"Patience, *pethi mou*," he said with the twist of his lips.

Patience? She had not shared his bed for months. Her lips stung and her skin tingled for his touch. Her breasts felt heavy and full as she began to pant. She rocked her hips to alleviate the insistent throb. Couldn't Stergios sense her raging need? Of course he could.

"Is this payback?" she asked in a stuttering breath as he licked a path to her cleavage. "Because I made you wait?"

She felt his smile against her breast. "Would I do something like that?" he purred.

"Yes!" she said through clenched teeth.

He nipped her skin with his teeth. "I want to bury myself deep into you," he grounded out. "Hard and fast but I won't. I don't want to hurt you."

His words made her shiver with anticipation. She would break his restraint, she decided as she wrested for control. The straps of her slip fell down her shoulders, revealing her breasts, as she tried to pull her wrists from his strong hold. But Stergios would not let go. From the determined gleam in his eye, she knew he would not surrender to the lust stampeding inside him.

Stergios dipped his head and captured her tight nipple with his mouth. Jodie closed her eyes and tipped her head back as she mewled with pleasure. Desire flooded her as he continued this sensual torment. She bucked against Stergios, begging for more.

He readjusted his grip on her wrists and glided one hand along the length of her body. When he cupped her sex she almost came undone at his possessive touch. "Open your eyes." His voice was rough with desire.

Jodie followed his command and her gaze connected with his. He stroked the wet folds of her sex before he dipped his finger inside. Her flesh gripped him tightly. He watched the pleasure chase across her face as he teased her, his eyes darkening with uncontrollable lust when she held nothing back.

He suddenly let go of her wrists and slid down her trembling body. Stergios draped her legs over his shoulders and pleasured her with his mouth. A keening cry escaped her throat as she clenched her thighs against Stergios. Her fingers dug into his hair as she encouraged him closer. His husky moans and her shallow gasps echoed in the room. Jodie went rigid as the ferocious climax stole her breath. Her body shook as the heat scorched through her.

She lay limp beneath Stergios, her lungs aching as she tried to catch her breath. Through heavy eyelids she watched him shove off his pajama bottoms. He gathered Jodie in his arms, his chest hot and damp to the touch, before he rolled over.

Jodie straddled his hips. Anticipation pulsed through her body when she felt his throbbing erection against her. She slowly sat up, dragging her hands down his broad chest.

She smiled when she saw the hungry glitter in Stergios's hooded gaze. His angular features were drawn tight as a ruddy color stained his high cheekbones. He could no longer control the pace.

Jodie reached for the hem of her slip and slowly removed it, inch by inch. His fingers flexed on her thighs as she stretched and rolled her hips. She barely heard Stergios's ragged breath over her pounding heart as she tossed her slip to the side.

Stergios reached up and roughly caressed her body, molding her curves. She grasped his erection and he bucked against her. She stroked him and his growl was low in his throat as he dug his fingers against her hips.

Jodie guided him inside her. She smiled, her heart overflowing, as she felt his shaky restraint. Heat poured from her as he stretched and filled her. She rocked her hips, the pleasure coiling tight inside her. Her rhythm increased as she watched Stergios's face. Words spilled from her mouth unheeded as she rode him harder. Faster.

She cried out when the hot coil of need burst wildly and pleasure radiated from her core, streaming through her body. Stergios sat up and clasped her against him. Her nipples rubbed against his hairy chest as he held her in a tight embrace.

Love poured through her and she whispered against his ear, chanting his name. Stergios went still before he thrust wildly. She laid her head against his shoulder and clung to him before she surrendered completely.

Later that morning Jodie stood on the beach and stared at the ocean. She stuffed her hands in her coat and hunched her shoulders as the wind whipped her hair. She felt the cold through her jeans but she didn't dare go back inside.

What had she said to Stergios? Jodie nervously bit her lip. So many thoughts had chased through her mind. She had felt loved and cherished. She hadn't felt that way before and the sensations had overwhelmed her. But had she said those words out loud? Her stomach twisted with dread. Had she declared her love for Stergios?

She didn't hear him approach until he stood behind her and wrapped his arms around her. Jodie jumped and gave a shriek.

"Don't," he told her as she tried to break free from his embrace.

"Don't what?"

"It has taken me weeks to get you back into my bed." His voice rumbled in her ear. "Don't find an excuse to leave it."

She stood stiffly in his arms. "I'm not."

"You revealed yourself to me, *pethi mou*." Stergios pressed his mouth against the back of her neck. "And now you need to hide."

Jodie clenched her teeth and gathered her courage before she turned to face him. Heat unfurled inside her when she saw his sexy rumpled state. The dark sweater skimmed his lean body and the faded jeans clung to his powerful thighs. The shadow of a beard covering his jaw gave him a rakish edge. But it was his enigmatic brown eyes that made her want to take a step back.

She thrust out her chin. "I don't know what you're talking about."

He captured her gaze and wouldn't let go. "You told me that you love me."

Embarrassment pricked at her skin. Jodie felt the muscles twitching in her face as she tried to maintain an impassive expression. She had almost convinced herself that she hadn't said it out loud because Stergios had shown no reaction. But he had responded. He had gone completely still before he claimed her with a savage wildness.

His restraint had cracked because he knew he had won. He had complete power over her body and her heart. Jodie felt the flush creep up her throat and Stergios watched with a knowing smile as the color flooded her cheeks. She had bared her soul to him and had declared her love. How did she recover from that?

"It doesn't count when you say it while having sex," she said waspishly. "Everyone knows that."

"It counts when you say it."

He knew her very well but that didn't make her feel safe. She felt exposed and she had to get out of there. Jodie turned and trudged through the sand, wanting to get back to the house and get a few walls and doors between them. "Coming here was a mistake. We should return to Athens."

"Why? You weren't happy there," he called out to her. "That's my fault."

She stopped and turned around. "No, it's not. Why would you think that?"

"I thought that since I had included you in the family, everyone would accept you. I had underestimated how my relatives would react."

"It's not your fault," she insisted. "I can't seem to get along with your family. When I try, it just gets worse."

He splayed out his hands. "Why do you keep trying?"

"I don't know," she said with a shrug. "I always felt like the odd man out. I thought I would eventually win them over. It was a waste of time. It was always going to be me against them."

Stergios strode over to her. "I will always be on your side, Jodie."

Shock ripped through her. "Why?" It didn't make sense. He was an Antoniou. The leader of the family. "What if I'm in the wrong?"

"I'm going to take your side." He stood in front of her. "And you will take mine."

"Oh, now I see the catch." Jodie rolled her eyes and made a face. "But will you take my side when I don't marry you?"

"We're getting married." Satisfaction permeated his voice. "The sooner the better."

She drew her head back. "I haven't agreed to that. I won't."

"You said you wouldn't marry without love."

His lips tilted into a smile that made her heart skip a beat. "You love me."

Jodie clenched her hands at her sides as she fought the urge to wipe that smile off his face. "For the last time—"

He raised his eyebrows. "Are you saying you don't love me? Tell me the truth," he warned softly.

She snapped her mouth closed. She had made that promise to herself that she would always tell him the truth. Even if it didn't protect her.

Jodie felt jittery and cornered. She bent her head and walked to the water's edge. Stergios was at her side, quiet but alert. They strolled side by side for a few minutes as she tried to put the words together. "When I said that I would only marry for love, I meant that my husband would reciprocate how I feel. It shouldn't be one-sided."

Stergios gave a long-suffering sigh. "Why are you making this so complicated?"

"You're right. It is complicated," she declared, tossing her hands in the air. "Because if you say you love me, I won't believe you. I'll think it's because you need to get married and this was the quicker way to get results."

They fell into a tense silence as they walked on the sand. He eventually slowed to a stop and she stood beside him. When Stergios turned to her, she lifted her head to meet his inscrutable gaze.

"Jodie, you will get married out of love. I will get married out of duty to my family."

He clenched his jaw and a muscle bunched in his cheek. "You are in love with me but I don't love you. I can't."

Deep down she had always known this but it hurt to hear the words. She exhaled slowly as the pain bloomed inside her.

"I don't allow anyone that close to me. I never could, not since the kidnapping and finding out my father was behind it. However, I can pledge my commitment to you." His voice was low and earnest. "I will put you and our children first. Above all else. Above my relatives and my work."

He was making a vow to always respect and care for her. He promised to make her a priority. She wanted to believe him but she'd had too many promises broken to accept this vow at face value.

He reached for her hand. She found his fingers warm and steady. "I will protect and provide for you and our family. I will be faithful and I won't betray the love and trust you place on me."

She frowned at his solemn tone. Did he see her love as an obligation or a burden?

"And when you marry me, you will give me the same courtesy." His voice took a hard edge. "You will be faithful, you will protect our family, and you will put me and our children first. Do you think you can do that? Can you live that kind of life?"

Heaviness settled in her chest. This man knew her better than anyone else. He could offer commitment, family, protection and attention. Everything but love.

Why couldn't he give that, as well? She knew she was being greedy, but what was holding him back? What was it about her that he couldn't make that leap?

Jodie knew she shouldn't think that way. He was offering her a good deal but the disappointment pulled at her, trying to drag her down. Why was that? After all, when Stergios made a vow, it was unbreakable. How many women had a guarantee that their husband would put them first?

But was she willing to make a lifetime commitment to a man who could not love her? Give her love to her husband knowing that she would not get it in return? Could she enter a loveless marriage for the sake of her child?

"Yes, Stergios." Her mouth trembled as the tears burned her eyes. She had to accept, once and for all, that she was unlovable and nothing would change that. Now was not the time to be greedy. Why hold out for something that she could never have? "Let's get married."

CHAPTER SIXTEEN

STERGIOS STOOD IN the entrance hall of the Antoniou estate. He felt the bite of frustration as he looked for Jodie. Their engagement party was coming to a close and he was eager to have her to himself.

He should have been able to spot her instantly or hear her bold laugh from across the room. Dressed in a purple chiffon gown and wearing the Antoniou amethysts, his fiancée was an intriguing mix of a mischievous pixie and a regal queen.

Fiancée. Finally. There were moments when her stubbornness outmatched his tenacity, but she had accepted his proposal. Triumph and pride flared inside him along with the unfamiliar sense of satisfaction and peace.

Stergios shook his head. Peace was not related to Jodie Little. The woman tested him, pushed him to the limits. He didn't have to wear a mask around her and pretend. And yet, when he was with Jodie, he was the man he wanted to be.

His need for Jodie brought him little comfort. If anything, the knowledge had shaken him to the core. He knew better than to allow anyone that close to him but Jodie had slipped through his defenses. It was a constant struggle to maintain a wall between them when he ached to have her close. Was this what falling in love felt like? If so, he couldn't let that happen. For his own survival, no one should have that kind of power over him.

"Well, thankfully that is over," Mairi Antoniou said as she glided to his side. She wore a black evening gown that was the perfect backdrop to her diamond jewelry. "I hope the wedding happens soon."

"It will," he said as he took the last sip of his champagne. He was looking forward to starting his life with Jodie. Make everything official. He didn't want any delays.

"I don't think you should have given her that diamond ring for your engagement," his mother said from the side of her mouth. "It's an heirloom. It's priceless!"

"The wife of the Antoniou heir wears it. It's

tradition." And, more importantly, it meant that he recognized Jodie as family. As an Antoniou. A smile tugged on his mouth as he remembered giving it to Jodie. She had recognized the heirloom and understood the symbolism. She had been deeply honored. From the tears that had clung to her eyelashes when he'd placed it on her finger, the sense of tradition had meant something to her.

"But she'll try to keep the diamond when you two break up," Mairi insisted. "You need to get a written agreement that she gives it back in the divorce."

Sharp coldness invaded Stergios's chest. The more he had stayed on his island getaway, the more he had realized how his family had tried to chip away at his happiness with Jodie.

"I am not divorcing Jodie," he bit out. "She is part of this family—part of me—forever. Get used to the idea, *Mitera*."

She pursed her lips. "I know it's in poor taste to predict the divorce during the engagement party, but you have to agree—"

"If you can't support the idea of Jodie and your only son together, then you will see very little of me or your grandchild," he warned before he walked away.

Stergios ignored his mother's stuttering apology as he walked to the door leading to the garden. He wondered how Jodie had survived living in this house when everyone had expected the worst in her. It was no wonder she had become reluctant to marry into this family. And all this time they thought she was trying to become an Antoniou.

He would protect her from his family, Stergios decided as he walked onto the dark portico. He would demand that Jodie was treated with respect. She deserved no less.

As he stepped onto the portico, he immediately heard Dimos's voice. "How long have you had your eye on Stergios?"

He spotted his cousin standing next to Jodie on the terrace. He was prepared to intervene but something stopped him. He didn't like the confidential tone of Dimos's voice as if they were sharing secrets. He should be the only one who knew Jodie that intimately.

"I was hoping to get a moment of peace before I went back inside," Jodie said wearily. "Where's your wife? You're slurring your words and you should go home."

"I don't want to go home." Dimos's voice rose sharply. "I want to know how you could have chosen him. I had followed you around for years and all that time you wanted Stergios. Why?"

Stergios went still and he found himself waiting for Jodie's answer. He had done things he wasn't proud of but that didn't stop Jodie from loving him. He wanted to know why.

"He's cruel and barbaric," Dimos continued when Jodie didn't respond. "Ruthless. He thinks this is his castle and we are his minions. I don't know what promises he made when he bedded you—"

"Stergios is the best man I've ever known." Jodie's voice cut through Dimos's tirade. "He takes care of his own."

Stergios frowned. He wasn't a good man. At times he was a monster. Jodie knew that first-hand. But he was the best man—the only man for her.

"He is a man of his word," Jodie continued, her voice vibrating with emotion, "and he would do anything for his family. He is going to be an amazing husband and an extraordinary father. He has restored my faith in men and that is saying a lot."

"You could have had me," Dimos said bitterly. "It would have been a wild ride."

Stergios bunched his hands as he saw a mist of red. The idea of Dimos touching Jodie sickened him.

"No, I couldn't," she said in a withering tone. "And do you know why? Because you're right. It was always Stergios. There was no competition."

Dimos's laugh rang out in the dark garden. "You are delusional, Jodie. The man is only marrying you to claim his heir. He's going to get bored with you within a month and then he'll pursue the world's most beautiful women like he used to. A year from now he will dump you and the brat in some apartment far away from here."

"You don't know Stergios." Her voice wavered.

"No, *you* don't," Dimos argued. "He's telling you what you want to hear. You are infatuated with an illusion."

Stergios had heard enough. He didn't need anyone poisoning Jodie's mind. He walked past the stone column. "There you are, Jodie," he said as he watched them both jump guiltily. "It's late and you've been on your feet all day."

Jodie didn't glance at Dimos as she gathered her skirts in her hands and climbed the steps. She reached for Stergios's hand and laced her fingers with his. She didn't say anything as he escorted her inside. As they climbed the grand staircase to his bedroom suite, Stergios asked, "Was he bothering you?"

"He's a pest, nothing more."

"I could always transfer him." His mouth twisted as he thought of a list of unglamorous locations. "Somewhere cold and rainy."

Jodie gave a light chuckle. "It's a tempting offer. I can't believe you thought I was interested in him. He's immature and spoiled."

"He's also closer to your age, handsome and charming." He remembered how he'd considered Dimos a worthy opponent for Jodie's attention. At times it felt as if Jodie preferred his cousin's company. "He's very popular with the women."

"Is he? I'll take your word for it," she murmured as he opened the door to their bedroom suite. She reached for his bow tie and drew him into their room. "You were far too popular with the women at the party."

He liked the possessive quality of her voice. "No, all eyes were on you." Stergios lightly brushed his finger against her ear. "You were made for these stones."

She gave him a questioning look. "What is it about these amethysts? Is there a story behind them?"

"There is." And tonight he would tell her when they were in bed together. Heat flooded him as he imagined Jodie yielding underneath him, wearing only the amethyst earrings and necklace. "Have you heard about the Antoniou legend?" he asked as he kicked the door closed.

Jodie heard the helicopter descend on the island and her smile widened. Stergios was home. She swung the door open and ran lightly on the path. She couldn't wait to tell him how much the baby had kicked during the day. Maybe tonight Stergios would get a chance to feel the baby move.

"Stergios!" Her heart felt as though it was going to expand as she saw him walk down the steps. He was a commanding force in his pinstripe suit and red tie. She met him with a kiss and drew back when his mouth was slack against hers. "What's wrong?"

"I had an emergency meeting with the security team." He looked pale. Shaken. "They've informed me that there's a credible threat against you."

"Impossible," she said. She knew Stergios spent millions on security cameras, safety features and armored cars. He had put a four-guard detail on her whenever she left the island and he had mentioned getting her a body double to distract the aggressive paparazzi. "Why would anyone focus on me?"

He leaned closer and splayed his hand on her rounded belly. "You're carrying my child," he said thickly. "It's the best way to get back at me."

"What are the threats?"

He reluctantly pulled away, as if he wanted to keep shielding his child with his bare hands. "I'm not discussing it with you."

"Not..." Her mouth gaped as she watched him walk to the house. "I'm not delicate, Stergios. I have a right to know."

He held the door for her and ushered her inside. Once he closed the door he went straight to the drink cabinet. She watched him grab a shot glass and the clear bottle of Tsipouro. She knew the threats had gotten under his skin. She had remembered how troubled Stergios had been the last time he had reached for the potent liquor.

Jodie wrapped her arms around herself as she approached him. "Why would someone tell you what they're going to do? That ruins the element of surprise."

"They do it to instill fear." The drink splashed in the shot glass. "It's amazingly effective."

"How long have the threats been going on?" she asked.

He froze, the glass midway to his mouth. She wasn't sure he was going to answer. "After we made our first public appearance at the museum."

She exhaled slowly. "That long? And this is the first time you tell me?" She struggled to lower her voice. "You lecture me about not trusting you and you were hiding this?"

"I didn't want to worry you," he said before he downed the shot and grimaced.

Jodie shook her head. Stergios seemed to think that his need for security outweighed everything else. "So what are we going to do? Increase security?"

He paused and set the glass down hard as though it was a gavel. "I've decided that you're going back to New York. You will be far away from the threat," Stergios said as he walked to the window. He set his hands on his hips. "I'll have the security team look over your apartment and—"

"You want our baby born in Greece," she reminded him. Why was that no longer important? Her pulse fluttered with panic as she saw his grim face in the reflection. "You want me here."

"This is only temporary."

She tasted fear and swallowed hard. She hated that word. *Temporary.* It was vague. All of her homes had been temporary. She was finally feeling settled. This was becoming her home and now she had to leave. "What if it isn't?"

He was silent. Stergios didn't turn around. He didn't move.

Jodie raised her hand in defeat. "You know what? I'll go back to your mother's house. That place is a fortress."

"You are going back to New York if I have to drag you there."

She'd like to see him try! "What about the wedding?"

He gave a deep sigh and turned around. "We have to postpone it."

The panic that had bubbled inside her was now flowing over. All this time he wanted the security of marriage. Now he had changed his mind. No, she thought bitterly, it was just a postponement. It was *temporary*.

"Stergios, you have wealth, fame and power." She hated how weak her voice sounded. "That is going to attract the good and the bad in people. Once this threat fades, something else is going to replace it. You can't put your life on hold."

"I am not going to allow anything to happen to our child," Stergios said in a fierce growl.

"Neither will I," she promised. "But leaving home because one person made a threat? Why, when this island is well protected?"

Stergios raked his hands in his hair. It was as if he had gone through this argument several times before. "The security team thinks this is the best course."

"I disagree," she said as she clenched her jaw. "I think it's unreasonable. How are you going to conduct business from across the world?"

"The threat isn't focused on me," he said quietly.

Jodie tilted her head. She didn't like his carefully modulated tone. She was missing something. "You just said that this is probably a way to get to you."

His eyes were inscrutable. "I have to stay in Greece."

He wasn't coming with her. He was sending her away. Dimos's words echoed in her head. *He will dump you and the brat in some apartment far away from here.* She tried to block it out as her heartbeat roared in her ears. "I'm not leaving you."

"It's for your own protection."

"Stergios, don't do this, please." Jodie bit her lip. She knew better than to beg. Her fingers ached to grab his clothes and plead her case, but that would only drive him away. "I don't want to go."

He straightened his shoulders and clasped his

hands behind his back. “I wish it hadn’t come to this.”

“I don’t want to leave you.” She finally found that someone with whom she wanted to share her life. She belonged with him and Stergios belonged with her. “I want to stay here.”

“But I want you to go,” he said as the harsh lines in his face deepened. “I won’t forgive myself if anything happens to you or our child.”

I want you to go. The words sliced through her like a jagged knife. He wanted this so-called temporary separation. He wouldn’t miss her. Why should he? He didn’t love her.

Jodie’s legs shook and she thought she would fall into a heap at his feet. “When am I supposed to leave?”

He watched her carefully. It was obvious he didn’t trust her flat voice or her sudden acceptance of the situation. “The helicopter pilot is waiting for you.”

She felt the tears rolling onto her eyelashes. “Now?” Her voice cracked.

“I don’t want to give this guy any opportunity to hurt you.”

He was rushing her. Not giving her time to

think. He was treating her like an opponent, determined to win before she knew what hit her. "I'm not packed."

"You don't need much. You have an apartment in New York," he reminded her. "And you'll be back soon."

He's telling you what you want to hear. You are infatuated with an illusion. She knew why Dimos's words stuck with her. She had often been guilty of believing what she wanted to be true. How many times had she believed her parents' promises before they had shipped her off to school? They had given her hope because they had been tired of her tears and bargaining. The more she had protested, the more they drew away.

"Are you coming with me? Just to make sure I'm okay?" she asked. She wasn't ready to walk away from Stergios. Maybe she could convince him on the long plane ride that they would do better as a team.

A muscle twitched in his jaw. "It's not a good idea."

She felt like she was bleeding inside. "When will you come visit?"

"I don't know," he admitted in a gravelly voice.

She knew what that meant. He wouldn't visit her. He might contact her. At first there would be a flurry of phone calls and texts. There would be promises to visit soon and proclamations of missing her. And then it would start to taper off. There would be a series of missed calls. Unanswered texts.

Tears burned her eyes and she took short, choppy breaths. Jodie tried to tell herself not to expect the worst. Stergios was not like her parents. He promised a commitment. He promised that she would come first.

So why did it feel as though he was abandoning her? His life would go on while hers was put on pause. She was going to be uprooted and sent away.

Stergios glanced at his wristwatch. "We need to leave as soon as possible. I have a jet waiting for you at the airport."

He wasn't even lingering. She knew the threat scared him. It was like his nightmare coming to life. She needed to respect it and yet…would he send her away if he loved her? Would he insist on this separation if he couldn't live without her?

She didn't know why she was torturing herself

with these questions. She needed to accept the truth. He could live without her.

Jodie staggered back as the truth pierced her. She needed to protect herself before she splintered into pieces. “I’ll go get my passport.”

Stergios’s relief was palpable as she walked to the bedroom. She felt stunned and yet she was aware of her surroundings. She heard him reach for his cell phone before he spoke in a low, urgent tone.

Once Jodie closed the bedroom door, she walked to the middle of the room and stopped. She looked down at her engagement ring. It represented hope and commitment. Promises and family. But it had all been an illusion.

The tears clogged her throat as she pulled the ring off and placed it on the table by the bed. If Stergios wanted her back, if he wanted to marry her, then he was going to find her in New York and convince her to return.

Because right now, she was better off on her own.

CHAPTER SEVENTEEN

STERGIOS SAT ALONE in the ornate living room in Jodie's Upper East Side apartment as he waited for her return. He hadn't seen her in over a week and he had been in quiet agony. His life had been in disorder and he wanted his fiancée back.

He wasn't certain of his welcome. On his flight over, he had imagined that she was at home, pining for him. But the surprise was on him. Jodie had plunged back into her full social life as if she had to make up for lost time.

Stergios heard the front door open and he sat up straight in his chair. Anticipation beat wildly inside him when he heard Jodie's familiar voice as she spoke on her cell phone.

"Yes!" Her laugh made his heart take a tumble. "We definitely should meet up, Henry. It's been a long time."

Henry? Hot, bitter jealousy rolled through him and he clenched the armrest with his fingers.

Who was Henry? The security team had not mentioned this man. And why did she sound so happy talking to this Henry?

He saw Jodie stride past the door and her cheerful voice faltered. Stergios didn't move as he waited. He kept his steady gaze on the doorway and watched her slowly retrace her steps.

Jodie looked radiant and healthy as she stood at the threshold. Her gray dress acknowledged but didn't accentuate her full breasts and pregnant belly. Her red lips parted open but she didn't smile. Her blue eyes sparkled with surprise and joy but immediately went blank.

"Let me call you back," she said in a trance before she disconnected the call. She lowered her hand and stood as still as a statue. "The security team didn't tell me you were here," she said through bloodless lips. "I guess we know where their loyalties lie."

"Who is Henry?" Stergios winced at his harsh tone. This was not the reunion he had intended.

"An old friend." She tossed her phone on a nearby table and leaned against the door frame. "And what have you done to my butler and my housekeeper?"

"I've given them the day off."

She arched her eyebrow with displeasure. "What brings you to New York?"

"You," he said in a husky purr. He didn't want to spend another day without her.

"Isn't it dangerous to be near me?" She pursed her lips as though she was holding back what she really wanted to say. "Wasn't that why you sent me away?"

He heard the hurt weighing down her voice. "We caught the man who made the threats. He has a history of stalking celebrities and public figures."

"So it's over." She gave a sharp, decisive nod and crossed her arms. "Thanks for letting me know. There was no reason to fly all the way over here. You could have left word with your security team."

She showed no joy or relief like he had when he'd received the news. He had rushed over to America the moment it was safe and she didn't feel the need to cross the room for him. "I'm here to take you back home."

She motioned at the ornate walls and painted ceilings. "I am home."

This was not her home. She didn't stamp her personality anywhere in this four-bedroom penthouse apartment. It was as impersonal as a hotel room.

"You have a nursery to finish and we can get back to our wedding plans. Which reminds me." He reached into the breast pocket of his jacket and held the diamond solitaire between his fingers. "You left this behind."

He had been stunned to discover that Jodie had removed her engagement ring before she left Greece. Panic swelled deep inside him when Jodie stared wordlessly at the ring.

She glanced up and her gaze collided with his. "It no longer belongs to me," she said in a hoarse whisper.

Stergios jumped from his seat and gripped the ring in his hands. "What the hell is that supposed to mean?"

She thrust out her chin. "It means that I'm not returning to Greece and I'm not returning to you."

He was losing her. The diamond bit his palm. Stergios drew in a short breath as alarm squeezed his chest. He had realized how much he needed her when they were apart. Now he couldn't get her back. "Why?"

"Why?" Anger flashed in her blue eyes as she pushed away from the door frame. "How can you ask that? You shipped me off at the first excuse."

"It was not an excuse!"

"If you are going to send me away every time there's a problem, then it's better if I stay here in New York."

"That is not going to happen. You made promises and—"

"So did you," she lashed out and pointed accusingly at him.

He sliced his hands in the air. "We are getting married. The sooner the better." He needed to bind Jodie to him in every possible way.

"No." She waved her hands and took a step back. "I will still give you full access with the baby but not with me. That's over."

"Because I tried to keep you safe?" His voice rose in disbelief.

"Because you cast me off the first chance you got." She glared at him as the hurt shimmered from her eyes. "Because you disregarded my fears in favor of yours."

"That's not what happened." Or had it? He remembered her pleas when he had sent her away. He had wanted to give in and hold her in his arms, but he had known he had to stay strong. This time he hadn't been able to let her have her way.

"Do you think I felt safe when I was sent away and I didn't know for how long?" Her bright red lips trembled. "Am I supposed to feel some sort of security when I'm isolated and I don't hear from you?"

"I didn't call you right away because of security reasons. I didn't want you to be located. And then when I tried to contact you I couldn't reach you."

She hastily wiped her eyes with the back of her hand. "I've heard every excuse when my parents didn't stay in contact with me, but that's a new one."

He splayed his hands out as the anger and frustration billowed inside him. "Do you think I wanted to stay away from you?"

"Yes."

The simple word was like a punch in the stomach. How could she believe that?

"I made the most difficult decision to let you

go," he said gruffly. "I didn't know how long it would be until I saw you. I denied myself the pleasure of watching our child grow strong inside you. I knew it was a possibility that I would miss every milestone of this pregnancy and very possibly the birth. But I made that choice because I needed to keep you safe."

"But you didn't allow me a choice," she argued, her eyes flashing with fire. "You didn't give me any information or time to make a decision."

"The less you knew about the threats—"

"No, you don't get to say that. You made these decisions because you knew you had power over me. I have rarely refused you anything and that is my fault. I settled for commitment over love and this is where it got me." A tear tracked down her cheek. "Alone and abandoned."

He was suddenly in front of her. "Jodie," he said in a ragged breath as he reached out and rubbed the tear away. Her pain was ripping him apart. He had hurt her without realizing it. He did this. And he didn't know how to fix it.

"I trusted you but you took advantage of the love I have for you." More tears spilled over her lashes. "You know my history. You know how miserable I was having no family connection, hating how I was forgotten and invisible. And yet you did the same to me as my parents."

"It's not the same," he said as he cupped her face between his hands.

"Why did your fears take precedence over mine?" she whispered.

"The situation was urgent and—"

She pulled away from him. "The situation is always going to be urgent. Each separation will be temporary. That is, until it becomes routine. And eventually, I will be living away, alone and forgotten, because I had put my trust in you."

"I won't let that happen," he promised. Stergios needed another chance to prove that he was worthy of her trust.

"It won't happen because I'm not going to give you that power again. I won't allow you to decide my fate." She rubbed her hands over her face and rolled her shoulders back before she took a deep breath. "I will not marry you. We are co-parents and that's it. That's all you wanted, anyway."

"I want more," he said gruffly. "I want it all."

Her mouth twisted into a bitter smile. "So did

I. It didn't work out. Goodbye, Stergios," she said with a hitch in her voice.

The cold fear threatened to break him. Jodie was giving up on him. On them. He couldn't let that happen. "No, I'm staying here."

"Why now?" she asked tearfully. "Why not when I wanted you with me? Never mind. It doesn't matter anymore." She dismissed her questions with the wave of her hand. "New York City is big enough for the both of us."

"I'm staying here with you in your apartment."

She bristled at his commanding tone. "No, you're not!"

"We're co-parents, remember? You won't deny me access to my child." He sounded more confident than he felt. Stergios knew he was taking a big gamble. Jodie could strike back by keeping him away during the rest of her pregnancy. But he didn't think she would do that, no matter how hurt and angry she was with him. It was more important to her that their child had a strong bond with both parents.

"You're right, I won't," she said as her shoulders sagged with defeat. "That is the only reason I'm agreeing to this. I'll have the housekeeper make up a bed for you and you can have the library as your office."

"That's generous of you," he said softly as he watched her with suspicion. He thought he would have to fight tooth and nail for Jodie to make room for him.

"Only because I know it will be temporary," she said as she walked out of the room. "You'll leave and return to your old life once you realize that I'm not marrying you."

She had to give Stergios credit, Jodie thought as she swept into her penthouse apartment three weeks later. The man was determined to prove her wrong. He had invaded her home, her life and her every waking moment.

She tensed as his hands caressed her bare arms as he removed her coat. Stergios was a charming companion at the breakfast table and a supportive father-to-be at the doctor's office. He was the perfect escort to social events. She flicked her gaze at him, noting how sophisticated and sexy he appeared in his dark suit and tie.

He wasn't leaving, Jodie realized. At first she thought it was simply a battle of wills but now that she had put all the pieces together, she knew he was setting down roots here.

It didn't make sense, she decided as she marched away, her black cocktail dress swishing against her knees. He had other commitments. He couldn't stay in New York.

"You are in a bad mood," Stergios drawled as he followed her into the living room. "What's wrong?"

"I'm not moody," she said through clenched teeth. "I'm pregnant."

"Is it because Henry spent most of the time talking to me?" he teased. Her pulse gave a kick at his dazzling smile. "It's only because he wants another chance to beat me in squash."

"Who would have thought the two of you would have become fast friends?" she muttered. Stergios had made a point of meeting her closest friends during the past few weeks. They adored him and had loudly advised her to marry him before he got away.

Stergios shrugged. "Once I knew Henry wasn't a romantic rival, I could see that he's a good man who I could trust around you."

Jodie felt her nostrils flare as she tamped down

her annoyance. "I told you that he was an old friend."

"*Ne*, you did." He slowly turned and was suddenly in front of her. "However, what you didn't tell me was that he was the first boy who was caught in your room at boarding school."

"Oh, he told you that." She felt her cheeks burn under Stergios's possessive gaze. "Nothing happened between Henry and me. We're just friends and we looked out for each other. No big deal."

"He still looks out for you." Stergios paused thoughtfully before he continued. "Which is why I asked him to watch over you while I'm gone."

She flinched and she felt the blood drain from her face. "Gone?"

"I have to go to Athens for a few days." His tone was careful as he cupped her shoulders with his big, warm hands. "I want you to come with me but you've made it clear that you won't leave New York."

Jodie didn't want him to go. What if he chose not to come back? She was suddenly tempted to go on the trip with him but bit her lip before she revealed that to Stergios. "Why are you returning to Greece?"

His fingers flexed. She sensed that he wanted to gather her in his arms but he didn't move. "That's something I want to talk about with you. I'm prepared to step away from my position in the Antoniou Group."

Shock pulsed through her and she jerked out of his hold. "What? Why?"

He slid his hands in his pockets and watched her through hooded eyes. "It's the only way I can stay here with you."

"No, no, no." She raised her hands to stop him from that dangerous train of thought. "You can't do that. I won't let you."

"I can't abandon all of my responsibilities. I will stay on with the Antoniou Group as an advisor."

He wasn't listening to her. Jodie grabbed his arm. "Don't do it. You'll regret it."

He covered her hand with his. "*Oxi*, I won't." His voice was soft but confident.

"Maybe you won't regret it for a month or even a year, but you will one day." Her fingers dug into his sleeve. "You are giving up everything you've worked your entire life for. I can't let you do that."

Stergios's eyes darkened. "I know what I want, Jodie. It's you."

He was wrong. She bent her head as the chaotic emotions rushed through her. Stergios wanted access to the baby. He wanted to create a stable family life for his children. He didn't want *her*.

"Go back to Greece, Stergios." It hurt to say those words. Jodie closed her eyes as the pain tore through her. "Marry the heiress who can give you power. Rule the world. You don't need to stay here. I'll be fine."

"I choose you, Jodie." He wrapped his arm around her waist and drew her closer. "Why does that scare you?"

"You don't understand," she said in a whisper as her body went limp. "I'm not going to be enough for you. I'm not going to meet your expectations. I'm not the wife you need. I'm *keeping* you from what you need. What you really want."

"I need you," he insisted. His fingers spread through her hair and he cupped the back of her head.

"You are so far away from your home. You're not there because of me."

"I choose to live here." He tilted her head back and she had to meet his gaze. "This is where we can protect our relationship and no one with an agenda can tear it down. This is where you are valued and respected."

Tears burned the back of her eyes. "Your family is halfway around the world. You should be with them."

"You are my family." Sincerity rang in his voice. "You and this little one."

"But what about your goal to make the Antonious untouchable?" It had been the one thing that motivated him through his life. He couldn't give that up now.

"I will always provide for you," he promised. "I will protect you no matter what. But I will not spend another day without you," he vowed. "I want to fill my days and nights with you. I want to know our children and I—"

"When did you decide this?"

"When I sent you away to the other side of the world." The lines in his face deepened with misery as he remembered. "It was the wrong choice and I won't do it again. I promise we will face any obstacle, any threat, together."

"Why?" she asked breathlessly.

"I can't live without you. I don't want to anymore." His hand tightened in her hair. "I love you, Jodie."

She had yearned to hear those words and now she was afraid to accept them. If they weren't true, if his love wasn't strong enough to last forever, it would destroy her. "No, you don't," she whispered. "You told me that you would never—"

"I didn't want to believe it. I wanted to protect myself from being vulnerable," he said as he pressed his mouth against her hair. "I don't let anyone close to me, but I let you. Because I know you will protect me like I will protect you."

He loved her. Stergios loved her. Her breath caught in her lungs but she struggled to accept that as truth.

"I've been falling in love with you all this time. It's you. It's always been you," he confessed as he brushed his lip against her cheek. "And I'm going to prove my love to you every day. Just give me another chance."

She wanted to give him a chance but this was the biggest risk she'd ever take. If she took this leap of faith, it required her to be bold. Live and love wildly. She would accept his ring and take his name. She would create a family and a life with this man.

"Please, Jodie." His mouth pressed against her jaw. "Let me show you how much you mean to me. Let me love you."

"Yes, Stergios." She clasped her hands on his cheeks. "I want all of that and more."

EPILOGUE

JODIE SAT ON the stone bench and tilted her head back as the evening breeze carried the heavy scent of flowers. She inhaled deeply and smiled as a sense of peace washed over her. The splendor of the Antoniou estate gardens was lost on her boisterous and inquisitive children, who were now fast asleep in the nursery under the watchful eye of their beloved nanny.

It was a constant source of amazement for Jodie that she was a welcomed guest at the Antoniou home. Over the years the haunted look faded from Stergios's eyes and Mairi had gradually accepted that Jodie was the woman her son needed. Jodie was also beginning to see signs that Mairi and Gregory would be the kind of grandparents she'd hoped for her children.

Rising from the bench, Jodie brushed a leaf from her dinner dress and walked back toward the house. As she took a turn, her heart leaped with joy when she saw her husband striding down the path. Her gaze greedily roamed his body as she noticed how the dark suit emphasized his athletic build.

"There you are," he muttered as he reached for her. His touch was possessive and urgent as he clasped his hands on her hips and pulled her close. "I had back-to-back meetings but you were on my mind all day."

"Stergios!" She frantically pushed at his audacious hands but he managed to capture her fingers. "Someone will see us."

"I don't care." His voice was low and seductive as and he guided her off the gravel path. "I can't get enough of you."

Her spine bumped against the rough bark of a tree. Anticipation fluttered in Jodie's stomach when she saw the glitter of lust in Stergios's eyes. "Your family will think I'm a bad influence on you."

"They believe you've tamed me. Domesticated me." He raised her arms above her head, holding her wrists against the tree trunk. A slow wicked smile pulled at his lips. "If they only knew the truth…"

Her skin flushed as she remembered how she'd driven him to the height of ecstasy just before dawn. His response had been aggressive and primal as she'd held him spellbound. "Mairi will banish me from this house," Jodie warned as she arched against Stergios.

"I go where you go," he reminded her in a husky growl. Stergios leaned into her and she yielded against his hard, masculine body. He teased her with the featherlight touch of his mouth as she tried to capture his tongue.

"You drive me wild," Jodie confessed as she tore out of his grasp and thrust her hands into his dark hair before she kissed him with a rapidly building hunger.

They had been married for five years and her desire for Stergios burned brighter than on her wedding day. Every intimate touch, heated debate and unguarded moment brought them closer. Jodie trusted this man with her heart, her body and her most private thoughts.

"And to think I had wanted a shy and compliant wife," Stergios murmured as he bunched the hem of her dress in his hands. "A woman who wouldn't distract me."

"You're the one who changed the course of my life. I didn't know I could be this happy." She hesitated and whispered, "It frightens me sometimes."

Stergios lifted his head. "Because you're afraid it won't last?" he asked as he let go of her crushed dress. "That someone or something will try to steal your happiness and destroy it. Or are you afraid of what you will do to protect your happiness?"

"All of it." Jodie looked away. "Am I that transparent?"

"Only to me." He gently cupped her face with his large hands. Her breath caught in her throat as he held her gaze with his intense brown eyes. "Because I know how you feel. It scares me how much I need you in my life. I will do anything to protect this. To protect us."

"I know." He had proven it to her throughout the years. They both had made choices, sacrifices and compromises in the name of love. "But one day we will be tested."

"Then we will face it together, *pethi mou*. When I'm weak, you will be strong for the both of us. When you're scared, I will protect you. I will be with you during your best and worst moments. And through it all, nothing will stop me from loving you," Stergios vowed before he claimed her mouth with a ravenous kiss. "Nothing."

* * * * *

Look out for more stories in the
ONE NIGHT WITH CONSEQUENCES
miniseries in July 2016

A VOW TO SECURE HIS LEGACY
by Annie West

BOUND TO THE TUSCAN BILLIONAIRE
by Susan Stephens

MILLS & BOON®

Large Print – July 2016

The Italian's Ruthless Seduction
Miranda Lee

Awakened by Her Desert Captor
Abby Green

A Forbidden Temptation
Anne Mather

A Vow to Secure His Legacy
Annie West

Carrying the King's Pride
Jennifer Hayward

Bound to the Tuscan Billionaire
Susan Stephens

Required to Wear the Tycoon's Ring
Maggie Cox

The Greek's Ready-Made Wife
Jennifer Faye

Crown Prince's Chosen Bride
Kandy Shepherd

Billionaire, Boss...Bridegroom?
Kate Hardy

Married for Their Miracle Baby
Soraya Lane

0616 Rom LP